Gigolo Johnny Wells

LAWRENCE BLOCK
writing as Andrew Shaw

GIGOLO JOHNNY WELLS

LAWRENCE BLOCK writing as ANDREW SHAW

Copyright © 1961 Lawrence Block

All Rights Reserved.

This is a work of fiction. Names, characters, places, and incidents are the products of the author's imagination or are used fictitiously. Any resemblance to actual events, locales, or persons is entirely coincidental.

Cover and Interior Design by QA Productions

A LAWRENCE BLOCK PRODUCTION

Classic Erotica

---

21 Gay Street
Candy
Gigolo Johnny Wells
April North
Carla
A Strange Kind of Love
Campus Tramp
Community of Women
Born to be Bad
College for Sinners
Of Shame and Joy
A Woman Must Love
The Adulterers
The Twisted Ones
High School Sex Club
I Sell Love
69 Barrow Street
Four Lives at the Crossroads
Circle of Sinners
A Girl Called Honey
Sin Hellcat
So Willing

Classic Erotica #3

GIGOLO JOHNNY WELLS

Lawrence Block

Chapter 1

The Seventh Avenue IRT pulled into the 96th Street station with a metallic screech. The doors opened. Six passengers left the third car from the front and made their way to the stairwell that would take them to the street.

There were two ladies in their fifties. One had a red bandana over her head and carried a black patent leather purse. The other was bare-headed and a shopping bag dangled from her left hand. There was a middle-aged man, small and featureless, who looked like an accountant. He carried a nine-by-twelve manila envelope under one arm and walked with measured steps. There was a teenage girl wearing false breasts and too much makeup, and her behind twitched as she ascended the flight of stairs. The movement was meant to be provocative but the girl succeeded only in burlesquing the motion. There was another girl, older, who looked like a prostitute on her day off. This was not unusual, since she was in fact a prostitute, and the day might be said to be her day off in that she worked only at night. She was returning now from an afternoon movie on 42nd Street. She went to the movies every afternoon and worked every night, except for four or five evenings each month when she took an enforced vacation.

There were those five—two old ladies, one man, one teenager and one professional slut.

And there was Johnny.

He was seventeen, but you would be hard put to guess his age by looking at him. He looked both older and younger depending on how you viewed him. If you saw the hardness around the well-spaced dark brown eyes, if you saw the tightness in the corners of the firm but full mouth, you might guess that he was in his mid-twenties. But then you noticed the almost too-easy walk, the cat-like way the long body moved with easy fluid grace. And his clothing—faded denim dungarees tight on his hips and legs, a still-shiny black leather jacket with zipper pockets—placed him again in his teens.

His name was Johnny Wells.

He mounted the stairs quickly and effortlessly and looked out at the intersection of Broadway and 96th Street. On the second floor of the building at his side was Manny Hess's pool hall. The boys were there now he guessed. Ricky and Long Sam and Beans, each with a cue in his hand and a gleam in his eyes. They weren't actually waiting for him, he knew, but he was expected. Now was the time to climb the flight of stairs which would creak under his feet, to nod briefly to those patrons and hangers-on whom he knew, to take a heavy cue from the stand and run off a quick thirty points of straight pool with the boys.

He didn't feel like it.

To begin with, he was too damn hungry to care much about pool or Ricky and Long Sam and Beans or anything else except filling his stomach as quickly as possible. He'd been prowling around downtown all day long and he was fed up with the hollow feeling in his stomach. He needed a decent meal and he needed it in a hurry. There were other things that would come afterward, more important things, but it was impossible to concentrate on anything else when you were hungry. Food first—then the rest.

He dipped a hand into the pocket of his blue jeans. There was a jingle of coins but he missed the rustle of currency. You could keep the coins, he thought. Stick to the folding green, lots of long crisp bills, and to hell with the nickels and dimes and quarters. The crap about taking care of the pennies and the dollars would take care of themselves was crap and nothing but. That had been one of his old man's bits of brilliance, along with the penny-saved-is-a-penny-earned routine, and where had it gotten the old man?

The grave, he answered himself. When you never hauled down more than thirty bucks a week, you didn't save too many pennies. And no matter how well you took care of them, they were still pennies. And then the old man was dead, just as the old lady had been for eight years, and there weren't even enough pennies left to bury him properly. The city had taken care of that.

Johnny Wells pulled his hand out of his pocket and looked at the coins in it. There was a nickel and eight pennies. He counted them three times. Then, suddenly, he laughed wildly and threw the coins into the gutter.

To hell with the pennies!

He ignored the people who stared at him and strode away quickly. When there was no place else to go, it was time to go home. Not that home was worth the trouble it took to get there, he thought. But he might as well get his money's worth out of the place. He wouldn't be staying there much longer. He hadn't paid a nickel of the rent for the past six weeks and he wasn't going to pay now. In another day, he judged, the landlord would get around to changing the locks. That would leave him out in the cold.

Where was he going to stay then? And what was he going to use for money? Those were good questions, but he didn't worry about them. Something would turn up. Something always did turn up, if you were a sharp good-looking kid with an eye open for a quick couple of dollars and the guts to get ahead. If you went through with your eyes shut and your shoulders sagging, then you were going to take it on the chin all across the board. But a sharp kid never got licked. He came out on top.

His room was on the top floor of a run-down brownstone building on 99th Street between Columbus and Amsterdam. He went through the hallway and climbed four flights of stairs, following his nose. It was easy to follow your nose in his building. The second floor smelled of cabbage, the third floor of garlic, the fourth floor of booze. You could tell that a batch of Irish lived on the second floor, a slew of Italians on the third, and a couple of lushheads on the fourth. You could also tell that the occupants of the building were not exactly rolling in dough.

He took the stairs two at a time and hit the top floor without breathing hard. He was in good shape. That was one thing about the life he led, he thought. It kept a guy on the go, kept his muscles in shape. And there was no extra weight on his frame, not when he never had any extra food to stuff his guts with. His arms and legs were strong, his stomach flat without a spare ounce of tissue on it. His chest was firm and hard and well-muscled. He was in damned good shape.

He kicked open the door of his room, pleased that that bastard of a landlord hadn't gotten around to locking him out yet. Not that it would make a hell of a lot of difference. The room wasn't much—good for sleeping in and nothing more. There wasn't room to swing a cat in it, he thought, and he was a very swinging cat.

He smiled. That sounded nice.

The room was very small. Its one window faced the brick wall of a building on 98th Street, and the room was dark day or night. A covering of scarred and cracked linoleum topped most of the floor, but the linoleum had been cut poorly and didn't fit well. There was a single cot that sagged in the middle. The sheets were dirty since he never bothered to change them.

There was no chair in the room, only a single dresser with three drawers, two of which opened. The top of the dressers was scarred with burns from twenty or thirty years of forgotten cigarettes, many of them his own. His clothes hung from nails that some enterprising tenant had driven into the wall. There was no closet in the room.

A pigpen, he thought. Six bucks a week and not even worth that much. It would be a pleasure to leave the goddamned place. Wherever he wound up, it wouldn't be a hell of a lot worse than the place he was in now.

He kicked the door shut, then tossed himself down on the bed without taking the trouble to remove his shoes. What the hell— why keep the sheets clean? They'd be somebody else's problem soon enough anyway. What the hell concern were they of his? Why worry about them?

There were other things to worry about. Food, for example. That was the short-range problem, the immediate concern. And money; and a place to live. His last eight cents were scattered in the gutter at Broadway and 96th, waiting for some penny-pincher to pick them up and stow them away in a lockbox. Hell, eight cents wasn't going to do him any good. It cost almost double that for a ride in the lousy subway.

He needed money.

He grinned, thinking what his old man would have done. For his old man there was only one answer—you found a job and you worked. You worked your butt off for a buck an hour, but that was good clean work, the American way, and you were happy to get it.

Crap!

They could keep their jobs, he thought savagely. They could take them and stick them for all he cared. He needed money, all right, but he was damned if he was going to bust his hump and go hungry while he did it. To hell with that noise.

A smile spread on his face. There was an easier way to get money. There was always an easier way, if you had that necessary core of hipness that would rule out work and keep you grooving with enough bread in your pocket. Everybody had his own way. For Ricky it was pool. Ricky had a phenomenal talent that way. He knew just how bad to look without making it obvious that he was holding back, fluffing shots on purpose. Then when the heavy bread was on the table he made the shots and let the mark think he was making them with sheer luck. Eight-ball was Ricky's favorite game. He'd line up an easy shot, then shoot it wrong and sink a very hard shot, making it look like on accident. The sap walked away thinking Ricky was a rotten player with a horseshoe up his rear. But Ricky was the slickest guy with a cue on the Upper West Side.

Or take Beans. Beans's old lady taught him to boost from the supermarkets so they wouldn't go hungry. She was too busy lapping up the sauce to do her own stealing, so she taught Beans the tricks of the game. Beans learned well. He had a working arrangement with a Third Avenue hockshop owner, and once a week Beans made a trip to Third Avenue with a cab loaded up with goodies. He was silky smooth in a store. He never got caught.

Or Long Sam. Long Sam was a heavy, not too brilliant between the ears, but nail-tough. The neighborhood was gang turf and any one of the gang would have liked to have Sam on their side. But the four of them liked to swing by themselves. They had no use for the gang bit. And nobody ever bothered them.

Sam did a little mugging when things got tight. He was on expert. He never hit anybody hard, never took a chance on falling into a murder mess. The arm around the throat, a gentle love tap behind one ear, a quick grab for wallet and watch and it was all over. He had his own angle and he never missed.

Johnny yawned, scratched his head. He had his own angle, he thought. He was an expert, too—and it paid off for him when it had to. Everybody had to have an angle and he had his.

It was women.

He didn't know why it worked so well for him and he didn't care. He wasn't complaining. It was partly looks, he guessed, and partly self-confidence, and partly something you couldn't quite put your finger on. Whatever it was he wasn't going to kick it in the head. It worked fine for him.

For years women had been picking up tabs, paying the freight for him. Hell, all he had to do was give a broad a hard look and she was flat on her back. panting.

And they didn't have any complaints when he was done with them, either.

He closed his eyes, the smile growing wider and wider on his handsome face. He couldn't remember them all—there had been too many of them, for one thing, and for another most of them had not been worth remembering. He'd done his best to forget them as soon as he was walking out the door with his desires satisfied and his clothes buttoned up.

Now he was remembering the first one. It hadn't been so long ago, really. Not when you stopped to think about it. Just two years.

It seemed longer...

He was fifteen. He lived with his old man in a fourth-floor two-roomer on Columbus. His old man was between jobs. Every day Walter Wells went out to look for work. He had a small breakfast at seven-thirty and didn't eat again until he came home around six, his eyes downcast and his shoulders slumped. The unemployment money wasn't enough. And the job the old man was looking for didn't seem to turn up.

Johnny still went to school—it would be a year before the city decided he was old enough to kiss the books goodbye. But he didn't show up at school too often. He walked around the park instead, or sat over a lukewarm coke in the Garden Candy Shoppe, or stood on a street corner and felt important.

He also stole milk.

He happened to like milk. It was ice cold and it tasted good, and it was supposed to be healthy. You drank milk and you got strong—that was supposed to be the gimmick. He wasn't sure whether it worked or not. The strong-looking guys in the neighborhood mostly drank beer, although they said beer made a lush out of you. But he liked milk, and since his old man couldn't afford more than two or three quarts a week, he stole it.

This was easy enough. You got up early and you went out and found a building or two to work. Most people bought their milk at the market, but one or two in every building had a milkman deliver it. If you timed things right, you hit the apartment after the milkman had made his delivery and before the customers had dragged the milk inside. Then you picked up the carton of milk and got the hell out of there.

Only this time it didn't work.

He made two mistakes at once. For one thing, he hit an apartment that he'd been to just a week ago. For another thing, he got a late start that morning. He overslept, and it was eight-thirty by the time he was standing in front of a carton of milk.

He reached over for it. He just had his hand on the damn carton when the door opened.

There was a woman in the doorway.

"I'll be a son of a bitch," she said. "You're the little thief who's been swiping the milk. I got a baby to feed, you little rat. What's the idea?"

Like a slow motion movie he released the carton of milk and straightened up slowly. He thought of turning and getting the hell out of the building. That was his first impulse but he stifled it. She'd run after him, or start shouting or something, and it would be a mess.

Maybe he could bop her one. She didn't look too strong. A little punch in the head ought to take care of her, give him plenty of time to beat it. But that might not be too good. She lived less than a block away from him. She could run into him on the street and recognize him. Maybe she already knew who he was. It would mean taking a chance.

Besides, she probably wouldn't call the cops. Not for a stinking quart of milk, not with him just a young kid.

So he stood where he was.

"A brave one," she said. "You don't say much, do you? You got a name?"

He didn't answer her. She wasn't bad-looking, he noted with some surprise. Not Miss America, but not bad. He placed her age at thirty, give or take a year. Her face would pass and what he could see of her shape wasn't bad at all. She was wearing a cotton wrapper that didn't exactly put her on display. But he could see that her legs were good from ankles to knees, plump at the calves and smoothly shaved. And even the wrapper couldn't entirely conceal the thrust of her breasts.

"So you haven't got a name," she said. "Okay, No-Name. I guess that's what I'll have to call you, huh?"

"My name's Johnny."

She laughed aloud. "It talks," she said. "You like milk, Johnny? Nice cold milk?"

He shrugged.

"Maybe I could let you have a glass of milk, Johnny. I'm an easy girl to get along with."

"I don't want any."

"But you were trying to take mine, weren't you?"

"I was just looking at it," he said. "I wasn't looking to steal it or anything. I ain't a thief."

It was an obvious lie and he didn't care whether she believed it or not. But it bothered him when she laughed. She opened her mouth to laugh. She had full lips and she was wearing dark red lipstick. He wondered why she was wearing lipstick at eight-thirty in the morning. She didn't even have clothes on but she was wearing lipstick.

Her hair was combed, he noticed. Long yellow hair that reached almost to her shoulders.

Pretty hair.

"My husband works on the docks," she said. "The docks on the Hudson. Early in the morning he leaves the house. Gets out of here around seven and he's gone all day."

Johnny was lost. He knew that she was trying to tell him something but he couldn't figure out what it was all about. He was nervous and he shifted his weight from one foot to the other.

"I'm all alone all day," the woman said. "Just me and the kid. And the kid sleeps all day. I didn't want the little bastard in the first place, takes all my time and makes a wreck out of me. I thought I wouldn't get my figure back when I had the little bastard, you know, but it worked out. At least I think it worked out. It's hard to say."

Her hands toyed with the belt of the wrapper. The belt came undone and the wrapper slipped open. He had a glimpse of soft pink flesh and big breasts before she drew the wrapper closed.

He had never seen a girl's breasts before, had never had much experience with girls. Oh, he'd fooled around a little bit here and there the way all kids do. But nothing too much ever came of it. One time he and Ricky had messed around with a girl named

Mary Krauss. She'd let them feel the softness of her breasts through the tight sweater she wore, but when they tried to get their hands up her skirt the game had come to an end.

This was different.

He knew instinctively that something quite remarkable was going to happen. Like most teenage boys since the creation of the heavens and the earth, Johnny thought a great deal about sex. Now it was coming and he didn't know what to make of it.

And now the woman was smiling. "So lonely," she said. "Just me and the bastard kid. I could use some company."

The robe fell open again. This time the woman didn't draw it shut. Johnny saw big breasts, huge boobs tipped with large red nipples. He thought the woman's body was the most exciting thing he had ever seen in his life. He stared hard at her, devouring her with hungry eyes.

She didn't laugh this time. She reached out and took him by one arm and drew him into the apartment. He didn't resist. He had no desire to get away now.

"Inside," she murmured throatily. "I have nosey neighbors. Inside."

When they were inside she closed the door and turned to him. Once again she opened her robe and once again his eyes roamed over her warm female body. They traveled from the full breasts down over a slightly rounded stomach to her thighs.

"I bleach my hair," she said. "You don't mind, do you?"

He didn't mind.

"Now you can tell me," she said. "Did I get my figure back or didn't I?"

His eyes answered her.

"You're a nice boy, Johnny. A nice boy. You want to touch me a little?"

He couldn't move. Her hand caught his and pressed it to her breast. He felt the rounded warmth of it and his heart raced. He cupped the breast in his palm and fingered the nipple. When he played with it, the nipple grew stiff and stood out from her breast like a toy soldier standing at attention.

She moved his hand downward.

Downward—

When his fingers were touching the soft warmth of her she shivered with delight. Her own hands became active, fumbling with his dungarees. She touched him.

"Nice," she cooed. "So big and so strong. Did you ever have a girl before, Johnny?"

He shook his head.

"I'm going to teach you, Johnny. I'm going to teach you everything there is to know. Oh, you'll like it, Johnny. You'll like it so much you'll scream. It's the greatest thing in the world, the greatest thing there is. And I'm going to show you everything about it, all of it. I'm going to make a man out of you, Johnny my boy. Oh, God!"

She gave a quick shrug and the wrapper fell from her shoulders to the floor. She stepped backward, moving away from him and he started to lunge after her. He wanted her so badly that he could taste it. Before he'd had sexual desires, vague cravings that were hard to define. They were nothing like this. He had to have this woman or go mad.

"Wait," she said. "Wait."

He stopped.

"Now watch, Johnny. Look at me. Look at my body."

She began to move and he watched, dumbfounded. She turned this way and that, showing him each part of her body in turn. She turned her back to him and he looked at her taut buttocks, aching to take them in his strong hands and squeeze until she screamed. She faced him again and bent her body backwards, her feet placed wide apart on the floor. He stared at her.

"Now you," she said. "Take off your clothes, Johnny. Take off all of them. Even your shoes and socks. And do it slowly. I want to watch you."

He felt self-conscious doing a strip tease for her but he didn't have the strength to argue. He was wearing a striped jersey. He tugged it loose from his blue jeans, then pulled it over his head and dropped it to the floor.

He stopped then, feeling the heat of her eyes on him. They were burning into his chest.

"So pretty," she said. "Smooth and hairless. You should see my husband. Hair all over his chest. He looks more like an ape than a man. Hair on his back and shoulders. Not like you. Not beautiful like you."

He colored.

"More," she said "More."

He undid the belt of his jeans, then unbuttoned them. She had already taken care of the zipper. He stepped out of the jeans and left them in a heap on the floor. Again he had to stop. She was eating him alive with her eyes.

"Beautiful," she said. "So beautiful, Johnny. I could get hot just looking at you. Not an ounce of fat anywhere. My husband drinks beer all night. He's got a belly the size of the Empire State Building. Not like yours."

He looked at her again and saw her breasts. He wanted to have them in his hands again. His hands were sweating, itching to touch her.

"More, Johnny."

He kick off his tennis shoes, peeled off his sweat socks. Then he rolled down his shorts and stood nude before her. He was not embarrassed now. He was too excited to be at all embarrassed at the moment.

"You never did it before," she was murmuring. "I'm going to be the first with you, my young lover. Oh, I'm going to be good to you. I'm going to be perfect. And you're going to be good for me, little Johnny. Little? What am I talking about? There's nothing little about you, is there? Not at all. Big and strong. Come to mama, strong Johnny. Come with me. Come on."

He took her arm and they walked through a hallway to the bedroom. She pointed to a closed door on the way. "The kid's room," she said. "The little bastard of a kid I didn't want. That big bastard of a husband had to get drunk. He couldn't be careful what he was doing, so I've got the kid. I ought to bring him into the goddamned bedroom and let him watch."

They reached the bedroom. She brought him inside, closed the door, and melted into his arms. She was several inches taller than he was and he pressed his mouth to the side of her neck and kissed her. All of her body was pressed tight against all of him and the contact was electrifying. He felt her firm meaty breasts against his chest. His desire mounted higher from the contact with her sweet warmth.

"The bed, Johnny."

It was a double bed. She pushed the covers aside and stretched out on the top sheet on her back. She moved the pillows out of the way. "We don't need pillows," she whispered. "I'll be your pillow, Johnny. All soft for you."

He stretched out beside her, not sure just what he was supposed to do next. He kissed her and his mouth was forced open by her probing tongue. The tongue sank between his lips, past his teeth, and lit little fires all over the inside of his mouth. Her arms clutched him very tight and their bodies were pressed together. He was blinded by desire.

"My breasts," she moaned. "Kiss them, Johnny. Kiss them and play with them."

He bent over her and took a breast in his hands. He brought it to his mouth and pressed his lips to the warm sweet flesh. She didn't use perfume but she had something that was better than perfume. She smelled like a woman aroused to go. It wasn't a smell he recognized but he knew its significance at once.

His lips raced over her breasts. He kissed the nipples and her whole body began to shiver and shake.

"Kiss them, Johnny. As hard as you can—"

He kissed each nipple in turn, taking each tiny turret between his lips and working hard on it. He bit her experimentally once or twice and was rewarded with a small gasp of passion.

"Now touch me. There, that's right. God, that feels good. Oh, you don't know how good it feels. It's wonderful. It's the nicest feeling there is. Touch me some more. That's right, oh, God, it feels good it—"

His heart was beating like a trip hammer and his brain was

spinning dizzily. He was going to have her now. He was ready, she was ready, and—

She took hold of him. "Oh, touch me," she breathed. "But not with your hands, it's nice with your hands but that's enough now, enough with the hands, touch me with *this!* Oh, come on, come on Johnny baby, that's right, oh, yes, oh yes, oh that's right, that's the way, oh *God!*"

He fell on her, aching for her, and her breasts cushioned his fall. He had trouble for a moment but her hand helped him, following the directions on the accompanying printed sheet and neatly joining plug A to socket B.

Once the connection was made it damn near electrocuted both of them.

Her mouth was at his ear, kissing him, mumbling words of encouragement and endearment to him. Her thighs were locked around his hips in a death-grip that was life itself and her arms were taut as bands of structured steel around his chest.

They moved.

They moved together, and his body learned movements it had never known before. All at once he knew everything he was supposed to do and he did it flawlessly. She was an unobtrusive teacher, showing him things as they went along, teaching him little tricks that sent his blood boiling and that urged him on to bigger and better things.

He moved again and again and the world raced by them. It got better and better and he thought he was going to die from the sheer pleasure of it. It was like nothing he had ever dreamed of, nothing he could possibly have imagined. It was the most wonderful thing he had ever experienced, the most wonderful thing in the entire world.

It got increasingly better, until the height was reached by both of them at once. Together they exploded. Her legs squeezed him and nearly cut him in two. Her nails raked his back and drew blood. He never felt the pain.

He bit her shoulder. His hands were on her buttocks when it happened for them and he squeezed them so that they were black and blue for three days.

And she never felt the pain either.

Then it was over. Slowly the world came back to normal again. He lay with her for a long time, unable to move, and she didn't mind his weight. Finally after what seemed like at least a month, he moved away from her.

She sighed.

"Johnny," she whispered. "God. Johnny."

He didn't say anything. She stood up and slipped her slippers on, reached for another nightgown.

He opened his eyes and looked at her.

"Don't move," she said. "Don't do anything. Just stay there. I'll be right back."

His eyes questioned her.

"It's all right," she told him. "Just stay here. I have to go in the kitchen for a minute."

"To feed the kid?"

"To hell with the bastard," she snapped. "No, not to feed the kid. I'm going to bring you some milk. A whole goddamned quart of it."

•   •   •

She brought him the milk. And then they went back to bed together, twice more that morning, and she taught him things most men never learn if they live to be a hundred. He left her apartment exhausted, but a man.

He came back frequently after that. Always she had a glass of milk for him when he walked in the door and another after he made love to her.

On his third visit he learned that her name was Joan Barber. She had not volunteered the information before that and he had never thought of asking her. It didn't much matter to him what her name was.

Eventually she took to giving him a dollar or two when they were together. She handed him the money without saying anything and he took it without thanking her. He figured that that was the way their relationship was. She wanted him, and she knew that he didn't have much money. So she slipped him a dollar now and then.

For four months he saw her two or three times a week. They made phenomenal love during those four months. He learned a great deal—enough so that he could tell quickly what girls were ready for him and what ones were not. He managed to find four who were, during the time he was seeing Joan Barber. One had been a virgin before he got to her.

He changed that.

After four months his visits had dropped off to twice a week at the most, occasionally only once a week. Then one morning he went to her apartment and she wasn't there. He checked the next day and found out that she and her husband had moved to another apartment in another section of town.

He never saw her again. He didn't much care. As far as he was concerned she was just a broad, pure and simple. His first one, as it happened, but just a broad.

Chapter 2

He laughed, remembering the first time with Joan Barber. Christ, what a green punk he'd been! Well, there had to be a first time for everything. And that had been the first time for him. There was a lot of water over the dam since then.

His stomach reminded him that he was hungry. He sat upright on the bed, kneading his stomach with strong fingers. He guessed that it was about seven o'clock. It was late April and the air was warm out. He got up from the bed and left the room. He didn't even bother shutting the door after him. There was nothing there for anybody to steal.

He hurried down the stairs, taking them two at a time again and passing in rapid succession the smells of alcohol and garlic and cabbage. He left the building and felt in his pockets for a cigarette. There was only one Lucky left in the pack. He took it out and put it between his lips, then crumpled the pack and flipped it into 99th Street.

A cleaner New York is up to you, he thought scornfully. Cast your ballot here for a cleaner New York. And did you make New York dirty today?

Nuts, he thought. He found a pack of matches in another pocket, yanked one out and scratched it into flame, cupping his hands for the light. He sucked smoke into his lungs and exhaled.

He left the cigarette between his lips and headed down the street, his hands plunged into the pockets of his dungarees, his body loping easily as he walked.

Food.

A meal.

Money.

And their source: a woman.

He remembered the last woman and grimaced distastefully. She'd been old, with breasts that sagged to her waist. And she barely had a waist. It was almost as wide as her hips.

And that wasn't all that was too wide.

He hawked and spat. The woman wasn't the worst of it: She lived in a ratty apartment on Amsterdam and her brats were squalling away in the other room while they were going at it. The whole place reeked of cooking smells. And afterward, when she'd had the decency to go to sleep so he could go through her pocketbook, all he'd gotten for his trouble was a lousy five bucks.

That was the trouble with being broke, he thought. If he had enough dough saved up he could buy himself a front—a decent suit, a couple of shirts, a good pair of shoes. When you could come on fairly strong you weren't stuck with the neighborhood and old broken-down wives of longshoremen and truck drivers. You could go where the good pickings were.

59th Street, for example. He ran into a guy named Bernie a while back, a smoothie who dressed sharp and had a line you could hang your wash on. Bernie told him about the bars on 59th Street just south of the park. The classy East Side broads went there when they had an itch and needed somebody to scratch it for them. You sat down at the bar and ordered a drink. They'd give you the eye and you'd carry your drink to where they were and they'd slip you money for the next round. Then you played footsie and kneesie until the gal made up her mind that she was warm for your form and ready to play.

And you didn't go back to a dump on Columbus Avenue. If the broad didn't have a husband, or if the husband was out of town, you went to the broad's apartment. You banged the broad in a bed with silk sheets and you lapped up twenty-year-old brandy between sets. And the broad might not be classy, but she wouldn't be a mess. She'd have the best beauticians in the world taking care of her, and she'd look good even if she didn't have much to begin with.

He spat again. On top of that, you made money in the deal. Twenty bucks for a night was the minimum and Bernie said he got as much as fifty or a hundred from the right broad. And you didn't have to go through her purse for it. She slipped it to you just as cute as could be.

That wasn't all Bernie had had to say. Sometimes a broad would go nuts over a guy and want him around steady. Then he'd move in with her and she'd buy him hundred-dollar suits and twenty-dollar shoes and pick up all the tabs, with a little spending money thrown in. And the broads weren't necessarily pigs, not by any means. Or eighty years old. A friend of Bernie's had managed to latch onto a twenty-nine-year-old divorcee with red hair and a trim shape and the biggest pair of boobs in captivity. A good face, too. And she was keeping him. She'd even given him a Thunderbird to drive her around in. The car was in his name, too. It was his to keep, even if they split up.

Johnny threw his cigarette into the gutter. He could stand

something like that. You could get sick of living on the bottom all the time. To hell with the skim milk. It was too damned thin. It was about time he started lapping up some of the cream.

But first he needed money.

He walked the streets, looking for the woman who would buy him a meal. He wasn't looking for just any woman. It had to be one who was ready to play. Not just a broad who would let him give her a toss in the hay, but one who'd pay for the privilege.

He found her on Broadway between 100th and 101st Streets. He saw her coming the other way walking toward him, and he stopped walking toward her and leaned up against a lamp post, one foot crossed over the other and his arms hanging free and easy at his sides.

She looked at him. At once he raised his eyes to meet hers. He gazed very intently at her. He did not smile. He simply stared at her, telling her with his eyes that he knew everything there was to know about her and that he was ready to give her everything she needed.

He could tell that she understood the look. She was frightened at first—he saw that instantly—but the fear died quickly enough. She returned his glance, and her eyes said that she was accepting his challenge and ready to meet it. There was anger in her eyes, and fury, and hatred. But more than anything else there was desire.

He made his move with the simple assurance that was the product of long experience. He stepped forward, a false smile in his face, and called to her.

"Hi! I just got here myself. Didn't expect you'd be on time."

No one watching would have realized that they had never seen one another before in their lives.

She only hesitated for an instant. Then her face relaxed into a smile that was as painfully artificial as his own. "I'm glad I didn't keep you waiting," she said. He held out his arm for her and she took it. They started walking down Broadway together.

"That was cute," she said. "Very clever."

He shrugged.

"How could you tell? You must get your face slapped ten times a day."

"I don't come on like that unless I'm sure."

"And you were that certain of me?"

He shrugged again. Hell, he thought but didn't say, you had *bang me* scrawled on your forehead in letters an inch high. You're hotter than an old stove.

"Suppose you were wrong," she said. "Suppose I changed my mind. I almost did, you know. Suppose I got angry."

He turned his palms up. "Then I made a mistake. I thought you were somebody else. No sweat."

She didn't say anything. He turned his eyes and studied her. She was in her thirties, a fairly attractive woman not badly dressed. She was wearing a wedding ring on the fourth finger of her left hand. It was just a plain gold band, nothing fancy. He smiled, thinking that almost all the women he picked up wore wedding rings. And all the husbands wore horns.

"Where do we go?"

"Your place," he said. "That okay?"

"Yes. I suppose so."

"Where do you live?"

"On 68th Street." she said "Near Central Park West."

He whistled. "That's a distance," he said "What are you doing way the hell up there?"

"I work at Columbia University. In the library."

"That's up by 116th," he said. "You walk home every day?"

She colored. "I had nothing to do," she said. "I wanted to walk a ways. It helps me relax."

He didn't say anything.

"We don't have to walk," she said. "We could take a taxi."

"I'm hungry."

She looked at him.

"I'm hungry," he repeated. "Let's stop and have dinner first. Then we go to your place."

She didn't say anything. She looked away from him and he added, "You pay for dinner."

"Of course," she said, her voice tense. "I pay for dinner. I pay for everything, don't I?"

"That's the general idea."

She didn't say anything to that. He led her to a good medium-priced restaurant, the Blue Boar. It had been a much better restaurant twenty or thirty years ago when the Upper West Side had been an infinitely more desirable neighborhood than it was now. The restaurant was still good, with good food and pleasant surroundings. But the prices were lower.

"Is this all right?"

"Should be," he said. "I never ate here before."

They went inside. The manager's face said he was surprised to see a woman like her with a blue-jeaned leather-jacketed teenager. But he didn't say anything, leading them to a table in the rear.

"He gave us a look," she said.

"Probably thinks you're my mother."

She blushed and bit her lip. He grinned inwardly. This was a live one, he thought. He'd even managed to work her for dinner in a restaurant. She could have offered to cook for him at her place, but she didn't even seem to think of it. She might be good for a nice piece of change if he played his cards right. She lived in a pretty decent neighborhood and she dressed well.

Hell, he thought, she might even be a little fun in the rack. She's not too old. It might be a kick to give her a good one. She probably couldn't even remember what a real one felt like.

She ordered liver and bacon and he ordered a very rare sirloin. She didn't even balk when he picked the most expensive item on the menu. $4.95 and she didn't put up a squawk. This was going to be good. Even if all he got was the steak, it was worth it. He was starving.

He finished the steak before she was half-finished with her liver and bacon. He wolfed it down, gobbled his baked potato, emptied the glass of milk.

Then he asked her for a cigarette. She told him she didn't smoke and gave him thirty cents for the cigarette machine. He bought a pack and lit one, tucking the pack into his pocket.

She pushed her plate away. "Let's go," she said.

"You left half your food."

"I'm not hungry."

The hell you're not, he thought. You're hungry, but not for liver and bacon. You're hungry for me.

"You sure?"

She nodded.

"Hell," he said, "*I'm* hungry." He took her plate and finished her food in a few seconds, stuffing it into his mouth. It wasn't as good as the steak, but it was decent food. And when you were used to eating when you could, you didn't let anything go to waste. It was all energy. The more you ate, the longer it would be until you got hungry again.

She paid the check, leaving a dollar and a half for the waiter. When she had turned the other way he scooped up the bill and slipped it deftly into his pocket. Fifty cents, he thought, was plenty for the waiter. The other dollar was a dividend for Johnny Wells.

There was no dividend in the cab. She paid and tipped the driver herself when he let them off in front of her building, a brownstone a few doors from Central Park West. It was a brownstone like the one he lived in, but there the similarity ended. It wasn't the Ritz but it was fine. The building was very clean and in good repair. The hallway didn't smell of six different kinds of cooking. The stairs and hallways were carpeted.

Her apartment was one flight up on the second floor. A small brass nameplate on the door said Mr. and Mrs. David Nugent. He wondered idly where old Dave was. He hoped he was out for the evening. It would be a pain in the rear if he walked in at the wrong time.

That had happened once. Fortunately the irate hubby in that instance was a little punk with water on the brain. He had lunged at Johnny, furious, and Johnny had stopped what he was doing, bopped the guy calmly on the button and knocked him cold.

Then the goddamned broad had hauled him back down on top of her and they had taken up where they'd left off.

Mrs. David Nugent now opened the door with her key. They entered the apartment and she closed and bolted the door. The apartment was a nice one. The floor was carpeted from wall to wall and the furniture matched.

"Nice pad," he said.

"I'm glad you approve."

Her tone was icy and he knew that she hated him almost as much as she wanted him, maybe even more. He had to reverse the balance. He had to melt the ice, or all he was going to get for his trouble was the dinner. If they kept talking she was going to get control of herself and tell him to get out. He didn't want that to happen.

He could have made his play in the cab, but it might have been clumsy. Now, however, he was on sure ground.

He reached for her.

She started to back away but she was too slow. He caught her by the shoulders and pulled her close. When she tried to turn her head away he grabbed her brown hair with one hand while he held onto her with the other. He brought his mouth down on hers and ground a kiss against her lips.

At least the boobs are all hers, he thought. That was one thing. You could always tell padding as soon as you got up against it. Whatever this one had, this Mrs. David Nugent, it was all her own.

He held the kiss a long time. At first she fought him without much success. Then she relaxed and accepted the kiss but did not return it. It was like kissing a pillow.

Then she began to change. Very suddenly she sighed and he knew the battle was all over. She began to breathe more rapidly. Her mouth opened and his tongue entered it. Now she was returning his kiss. Instead of fighting him or trying to pull away she was pressing up against him, rubbing her body against his. She was no cold fish now. She was ready to go.

And he didn't have to pretend his own passion. It was good when they put up a battle, when you had to work on them and use a little bit of force. They were fun then. Now, for the first time, he really wanted her. It was a hell of a lot better when you really wanted a woman. Just going through the motions was an awful drag, but enjoying it was the greatest thing since the invention of the wheel.

He let go of her in the middle of the kiss and stepped away from her. He saw the look in her eyes, the way her mouth was open, the way she was breathing.

He smiled.

"Damn you," she said. Her voice was very bitter. "God damn you to hell."

"That's what you wanted, isn't it?"

She turned away. He grabbed her by the shoulders and spun her around to face him again. He was purposely a little rougher than he had to be with her.

"Well?" he demanded. "Isn't it?"

"I don't know. I don't know what I wanted."

"I do."

"What?"

"Bed," he said. "You want bed."

She clenched her teeth, closed her eyes for a moment, then forced herself to relax. "You know everything," she said. "You just know everything in the world. Damn you."

He pulled her close to him again and took her breast in his hand. He squeezed gently, then relaxed, then squeezed again.

"Go ahead," he said to her. "Tell me you don't want it."

She shuddered and said nothing.

"Now get your clothes off," he said. "Strip. In a hurry. Then we go to bed."

He stood with his hands on his hips while she wavered for a moment or two. He remained in that position and she began to remove her clothing. Her hands went behind her back to undo the zipper of her dress and the movement outlined her breasts against the fabric of the dress. She struggled with the zipper for a few seconds, then mastered it. The dress fell to her waist. She slipped out of it, then carried it to a wing chair and folded it neatly over the arm of the chair.

Then she came back and stood in front of him again. Now she was wearing a full slip, bra, stockings and shoes and panties. The slip was the first to go. It was a frilly white affair and he wanted to rip it from her body and tear it into a hundred pieces of soft fluff. But he restrained himself while she pulled the slip over her head and carried it to the wing chair.

She came back and took off her bra. She started to carry it to the chair.

"Hold it," he said. "I want to look at 'em."

She stopped, blushing, and he studied her breasts. They were much better than he expected. They were not large but they were perfectly formed, ivory mounds with saucy red tips. They looked to him like scoops of ice cream with maraschino cherries on top. There was no sag at all to them.

"Okay," he said. "Keep going."

She was moving like an automaton now. Numbly she took the bra to the chair, placed it over the arm, and returned. She unhooked her garter belt and rolled the stockings down over her long legs. The legs were not bad—a little on the thin side, maybe, but well shaped. And when a broad was on the wrong side of thirty, it was better for her to be too skinny than too fat. The fat ones got all flabby. Once their muscle tone was gone they weren't worth a damn.

She put the garter belt and stockings on the chair, then took off the panties. She was naked and he wanted her badly. He couldn't wait.

Without wasting any time he took off his own clothes. He burlesqued her ritual of placing each garment on the wing chair by ripping his clothes off and tossing them to the floor. He wanted to get the disrobing process over with as quickly as possible. She looked away while he got undressed.

"Look at me."

She turned and looked at him.

"Good enough?"

"Damn you," she said.

He laughed easily. "Now which way's the bedroom?"

"Through that door."

"Then let's go," he said. "Come on."

• • •

The bedroom was neat and feminine. The bed had a box-spring and an innerspring mattress and clean sheets. They lay down on it and he took her in his arms. Her teeth were clenched. She acted as though she was submitting to him because there was nothing else she could do.

He was going to change that. He was going to make her beg for it. Before he was done with her she would come on her knees to him if he wanted her to.

This was going to be good.

He held her in his arms and kissed her. Her body was cool, her skin very soft and smooth. He put one hand on her shoulder and ran it slowly and gently down her side until he was holding her bottom. She had a nice bottom, he decided, and he patted it gently.

He kissed her, still gentle, and her mouth opened for him. His tongue caressed her lips, rubbed over her teeth, dipped into her mouth. He worked very slowly, making all his movements gentle and calculating her responses meticulously. He leaned over her as he kissed her, lowering his body slowly so that his chest rubbed against her breasts for the shadow of a second. Then he raised his chest and broke contact.

After he'd kissed her mouth for several seconds he broke the kiss. He moved on the bed, then began to kiss her throat. The skin was very soft there. He kissed all over her throat, and he could feel the desire beginning to mount in her.

Mrs. Nugent, he thought, in a few minutes you're gonna be climbing the goddamned walls.

His hand found her breast and held it. He didn't manipulate the firm flesh, just held it in the palm of his hand. It fit perfectly.

He kissed her shoulder and his hand moved on her breast. He moved lower on the bed, leaving a trail of kisses from her shoulder to the very top of her breasts. He heard a sharp intake of breath. He was getting to her now. He was hitting home. He was finding the target.

He handled one breast as he began to kiss the other. Both his hand and his mouth were clever and skillful. The breasts were perfect and they excited him tremendously. It took effort to keep from tossing himself upon her there and then. But he wanted to take his time. He wanted to make it a good one, to drive her out of her mind with desire.

His lips kissed the underside of one breast while his thumb and forefinger played games with the nipple of the other breast. Then his mouth moved and he was kissing one pink nipple while he fingered the other one.

"Now," she moaned. "Now!"

He wanted to laugh. Already she was asking for it. Well, she was going to have to wait until he was ready. And he wouldn't be ready for a while yet.

"Now!"

But he wasn't ready to take her yet. Instead he let go of her breasts and moved downward, kissing her flat little stomach. He felt her whole body go tense with desire. He planted kisses all over her stomach, kisses that set her flesh on fire.

Then he skipped to her thighs.

Now she was burning for him. She couldn't lie still and she was squirming.

"Now! Damn you! Now!"

Not yet, he thought, not quite yet.

His lips moved, inching ever closer to their goal. The closer he got, the slower he forced himself to go until he was afraid she might go out of her mind any second, might flip completely and turn into a raving maniac.

He kissed with incredible skill while she wailed *Now Now Now* into his ears. He timed things flawlessly, driving her as close as he dared to the peak of passion without giving her the little push that would send her over the edge into a fit of satisfied ecstasy.

Then, when she was tottering on the brink, he let go of her and sat upright on the bed. He looked down at her, and he grinned.

Her face was a mask of pure hatred crossed with undeniable desire.

"Do it! Damn you, do it to me! Are you trying to kill me? Is that what you want?"

He laughed.

"Do it! Do it do it do it—"

"What do you want me to do?"

"*Make love to me!*"

"I don't understand you," he said carefully. "If you want it, you've got to ask for it right."

She didn't understand. So he told her the words to use, and she used them. He could have told her to do absolutely anything in the world and at that point she would have done it.

"Okay," he said. "Here it comes."

Then he fell on her, driving himself to her, and she gave a little moan of pleasure.

He used her cruelly and viciously and incredibly well. He sailed her to the top of the world and down again, and he took out everything upon her, using her body to give himself immeasurable pleasure.

It lasted a long time.

And then, finally, they came to the peak for the last time. His timing was perfect, again, and they got there together. He let his rage and passion explode with her.

Then they both were very still.

"You can go now."

He looked up at her, amused by her tone. It said that she was through with him, that he had served his purpose and that she was discarding him like a used napkin. He had news for her. But he dressed first before he told her about it.

She too was dressed. She had showered while he lay on the bed getting his strength back, and she looked neat and prim and proper. Only the dark circles under her eyes showed that she had spent a very energetic hour or so in bed.

When he had all his clothes on he checked his pockets, thinking that she might have slipped him some money while he was in bed. He found the dollar he had picked up from the tip, plus the pack of cigarettes. That was all he found.

"Hurrying to get rid of me," he said. "That's pretty cute. Your husband coming home?"

She stared at him. "I don't have a husband," she managed.

He laughed at her. "I can read," he said. "What happened to old Dave? Old Dave Nugent?"

She swallowed.

"He probably wouldn't like this," Johnny said. "You cheating on him like this. He'd be all upset."

"You rotten bastard. My husband died a little over a year ago," she said. "Do you think I'd step onto the same street with you if he were alive? We loved each other. He was a man, not a phallus with a body attached to it. You despicable—"

"So I made a mistake."

"Get out. Damn you, get out of here!"

"You owe me money."

She stared at him.

"Money," he said. "I don't give a damn why you wanted to get laid, but you got it and I haven't heard any complaints from you. So you might as well pay for it."

Her laughter was hysterical. "I don't believe it," she said. "You're not just a bastard. You're a whore too."

"Save the names. Just cough up the dough."

"How much do you get, whore? Five dollars? Ten dollars? What's your price, whore?"

He considered. He didn't want five or ten or twenty, not from her. He wanted more than that. He wanted the dough that would buy him a front, the dough that would put him in business. Dough for a suit, a place to live, a haircut and clothes and business expenses.

He wasn't going to get that kind of dough from her. But he *could*—if he was willing to take chances. How great a chance would he be taking?

"What's your price?"

He ignored her question, calculating the risk quickly. She

didn't know his name or where he lived. She didn't live in his neighborhood. She could describe him to the cops and tell them where he picked her up, but that was about all she could do.

And the odds were strong that she wouldn't say a word to anybody. She'd be pretty goddamned ashamed of what she'd done, and she'd be glad to be rid of him. She might miss him a little on cold nights, but she'd be happy enough never to see him again. That much was sure.

And this way he would get his stake. This way he would have that suit and those shirts and shoes, and a place to live and a foot in the door of every bar on 59th Street.

So why not?

"Well, whore."

The word didn't anger him. He wasn't at all angry when he hit her, but he couldn't have done a better job if he'd been madder than hell.

He drove his fist into the pit of her stomach. She doubled up in pain, not making a sound, and he hit her again. The second punch was an uppercut to the jaw, not too hard because he didn't want to knock her teeth out. Her teeth clicked together metallically and she was lifted six inches by the blow. Then she slumped to the floor and lay there in a heap. He checked her. She was unconscious, and she'd stay that way for a while.

He wasted no time at all. First he went through her purse in a hurry. He took sixty dollars in fives and tens from her wallet and found another dollar-eighty in silver plus three singles in a cloth change-purse. There were also six pennies in the change-purse but he left them there for her. He remembered the way he had thrown the nickel and eight pennies into the gutter that evening and grinned at the memory.

There was no more money in the living room bureau, but he struck pay dirt in the bedroom. The top drawer of her dresser contained another hundred dollars in twenties plus a small diamond solitaire engagement ring and a flat gold wristwatch with a black suede band. He got another less expensive watch from her wrist. He tried to take her wedding ring, more for the hell of it than because it was worth anything, but gave up when he saw that it fit too tightly. He could have cut her finger off, he thought, grinning, but that would be a little too much. What the hell— she'd been lots of fun in the rack.

He went through the apartment and took anything that was small and that could be converted easily into cash. He found a table lighter, a gold charm bracelet, a man's alligator billfold. It must have belonged to old Dave, he decided. He could use it to keep his own dough in.

He put the money in his new wallet and stuffed it into his back pocket. He hesitated at the door for a moment, then dipped into his pocket and came out with the dollar and eighty cents in silver. What the hell, he thought. So she can get to work tomorrow.

He looked at her. She was breathing normally, sound asleep and dead to the world. He jingled the coins in his hand, then tossed them underhand at her. A nickel glanced off the side of her face but she did not move.

"Live it up," he said to her. "And thanks. You've been swell."

Chapter 3

He hotfooted it over to Central Park West and crossed the street to get a cab heading uptown. The air was cooled now and he buttoned the leather jacket. A cab drew up and he hailed it. It pulled to the curb and he opened the door and slid into the back seat. "96th and Broadway," he said.

The cab started up and Johnny studied the driver. He was a small round-shouldered man with sad eyes and a weak mouth. Johnny guessed that the crumb would have given ten years off his life for a piece of Mrs. David Nugent. And he'd just had the broad for nothing. Hell, he'd come out miles ahead.

He took out the billfold, admired the leather, and counted the money. It came to one hundred sixty-three dollars. That was the cash alone, he reminded himself. The watches and the ring would bring more, plus the table lighter and the charm bracelet. Say an absolute minimum of a hundred clear for the stuff—and Beans could do better than that, he was sure of it. That made better than two and a half yards, which wasn't bad for a quick night's work.

It wasn't just the money, he thought. It was what he could do with it. He had the looks and the talent to make it in the Pretty Boy circuit. He'd needed the working capital and now he had that. There wouldn't be any more scrounging around on Broadway for a quick broad who'd pay for dinner and cough up another five when he twisted her arm. He could be choosy now. He could take his time and come on strong for a heavy score.

He was no dope. There were things he had to learn. You couldn't move where the big money was unless you knew how to act. You had to have manners and polish. You had to talk like a gentleman and act like one.

But those were things he could learn. You couldn't learn looks and you couldn't learn sex appeal. But if you had them to start with, plus a little gray matter upstairs, then you had it made. That guy Bernie—he hadn't been born with any spoon in his mouth. He was just a Rivington Street punk who played it smooth and got lucky. If he could do it, so could Johnny Wells.

Look out, world—here comes Johnny!

The cab dropped him at 96th and Broadway. The meter read seventy cents; Johnny gave the cabby a buck and told him to keep the change. What the hell, he thought—he could afford the thirty cents.

He hurried up the flight of stairs to the pool hall, hoping the guys were still there. He saw Ricky at a table on the far side busy proving that a fool and his money are quickly parted, especially over a table of eight-ball. The mark had a Joe College look about him and Johnny guessed that he was hot stuff at the pool table in the Columbia student lounge. But that didn't mean he could give any competition to a shark like Ricky.

He didn't say hello to Ricky, since that wouldn't have been too tactful while Ricky was fleecing the mark. It might tip things. Instead he nodded, and Rick flicked his head toward the back of the room. Johnny nodded in reply and headed for the back. Beans and Long Sam were playing rotation. Long Sam was working on the four ball. He had a one-cushion shot to play and he was lining it up carefully.

Beans gave him a nod. "We missed you," he said. "Pull up a cue and sit down. This game won't last long."

"I got to talk to you."

"To us or to me?"

"Just you. Nothing personal, Sam. It's in Beans's line of work is all."

Long Sam nodded. Johnny and Beans headed for the men's room. The pool room was a clean place; you didn't flash hot merchandise there and expect the management to love you. The two of them went into one of the booths in the john and locked the door.

"You got something to fence?"

"You read me right. Not just something. A couple things."

"Like what?"

Johnny took one watch and the charm bracelet out of his pocket. "Like this," he said. He reached in again and came up with the table lighter. "And like this." He tried another pocket and hauled out the other watch and the engagement ring. "And this."

Beans whistled "You scored heavy."

"That's about it."

"Where'd you get 'em?"

"Off a broad."

"Nice."

"Can you sell 'em?"

"Oh, no problem," Beans said. "This is the kind of stuff Moe likes for me to bring in. It's easy to turn over."

"What's it worth?"

Beans shook his head. "Hard to say." he said. "What it's worth and what it'll bring is two different things. Moe's an honest guy. I work with him regular and he pays fair because he knows me. But it's still tough to say. These watches could be worth ten bucks or two hundred and I couldn't tell you the difference."

"This one says seventeen jewels."

"Don't mean a thing, Johnny. You know what those jewels are?"

"Diamonds, aren't they?"

"Industrial diamonds," Beans said. "Worth eleven cents apiece. It can have twenty-one jewels and still be junk. It depends on the movement and the casing. And what you can get from Moe depends on how easy an item it is for him. One time I brought him a necklace he told me straight out was worth maybe four hundred retail. And he told me he couldn't give me more than thirty bucks for it. Something like that is tough to re-sell. He has to ship it to a guy across the country so it won't be identified by insurance guys."

"This stuff is safe," Johnny said. "The broad won't squeal. She wouldn't report me."

"Maybe not. But if she's insured you can bet she'll report the theft. She'll say it got burglared or something, but she'll report it."

"Maybe."

"So I don't know what I can get, Johnny."

"To hell with it," he said, shrugging. "You can sell it? You can turn it over tomorrow?"

"Sure."

"Take it now," Johnny said. "I'll meet you up here tomorrow night. I got things to do."

Beans stuffed the loot into his pockets. "I'll get what I can," he said. "You don't want to hang for a game or two?"

"No," Johnny said. "No, I can't. I got to move."

His own room was just as he had left it. He kicked the door shut and propped a two-by-four under the knob so that it wouldn't open. In a dump like that he wasn't taking any chances. Anybody saw he had better than a hundred bucks and he might be in for a rough time.

He didn't want a rough time. The two-by-four had stood him in good stead in the past; he used it as a lock whenever he had a broad up to the room. Now he had money, and that was more important than a broad. He sat down heavily on the bed and took the wallet from his pocket.

He counted the money four times.

A hundred and sixty-two goddam bucks. A beautiful hundred and beautiful sixty-two beautiful bucks.

It was more money than he'd ever had at one time in his life. It was a huge roll—and at the same time it wasn't enough to get going on until he got the extra dough from Beans. A suit alone would run him close to a yard all by itself. Shoes were fifteen or twenty, shirts five or six bucks apiece, socks a buck a pair. And he'd need an extra pair of pants and a sport jacket, plus a decent suitcase to keep his clothes in. You couldn't check into a hotel with a paper sack under your arm.

Then there was the hotel. If he was going to come on strong he wasn't going to live in a craphole. He'd need a hotel, and it would have to be at least average and probably better than that. That would cost money.

But if Beans brought back anywhere from a C-note on up, then he could swing it. And as soon as the front was set up he wouldn't have to worry about money. It would come in as fast as he needed it.

He smiled.

They'd pay, he thought. The goddamned broads would pay through the nose, just the way Fancy Pants Nugent had paid. They'd get what they paid for—he'd teach them what sex was all about and make them feel like a million dollars.

But they would pay for it.

He sat around planning until well past midnight. Then he stashed the alligator wallet between his mattress and the spring, pulled off his clothes and crawled into bed. He was tired now. The Nugent dame had been fun and the money was nice, but he was exhausted. She had really known how to wiggle that cute little rear of hers. She was choice stuff.

He smiled happily, remembering how it had been with her, how he had made her beg for it. They were going to do worse than beg, he thought. All the rich bitches with itches, they'd beg and more. They would come crawling to him, crawling on their hands and knees and crying like babies.

The picture pleased him.

He slept easily and well. He dreamed about money and women and power.

• • •

It was a few minutes past noon when he awoke. He didn't know this, though. He had no idea what time it was, and he realized that he was going to have to get a watch as soon as he could afford one. It was a shame Nugent's widow hadn't kept his watch as a souvenir. He would have kept it and worn it himself.

He got out of bed and his skin felt dirty. It wasn't surprising. He'd worked up a good sweat in the rack with the Nugent broad and he hadn't taken a shower since then. He wrapped himself up in a towel, grabbed a small chunk of dirty yellow soap and headed for the bathroom down the hall.

He opened the door without knocking, mainly because it never occurred to him that somebody might be inside. As far as he knew, nobody else in the stinking building ever got washed.

He opened the door and saw a flash of pink flesh. Then the pink flesh squealed and disappeared behind the shower curtain. The curtain was plastic and he could see a silhouette through it.

The silhouette was pleasantly female.

"Who is it?"

He recognized the voice. It was the girl who lived down the hall. Her first name was Linda and her last name was something unpronouncably Polish. She lived with her mother, a fat old slob who washed other people's floors and drank cheap wine.

He saw the bottles piled outside the door every morning. But he'd never paid any attention to Linda before. She was fourteen or so, which made her a little too young for Johnny to be interested in her.

Now, however, he wasn't so sure. What he had seen of her had been pleasantly pink. And the silhouette gave him a nice view of breasts that jutted out sharply from her young body.

Maybe—

"Johnny Wells," he said. "Sorry I charged in on you. You should have locked the door."

"The bolt broke."

He looked at it and saw that she was right.

"I'll be through in a minute or so," she said. "Then you can have the bathroom."

"Fine," he said.

"You can go now. I'll be done soon."

"Fine," he repeated. But he made no move to go and she didn't say anything.

What would the best move be? He smiled. He could take off all his clothes and step into the shower with her. That would scare the daylights out of her, but it ought to work. She'd be scared first, and then he'd grab her and give her a hug and she'd get excited, and from there it would be easy.

And fun. He could kill two birds with one stone. First they could soap each other up and have some fun in the process, and then he could turn off the shower and fill the tub with water and take her in it. It was supposed to be a kick in a bathtub.

Suddenly he was ashamed of himself. For Christ's sake, the broad was all of fourteen years old! What the hell was the matter with him?

Noiselessly he stepped out of the bathroom and closed the door. He padded back down the hall to his own room and waited there until he heard her open the door.

"All ready," she called.

He wrapped himself up in his towel again, picked up the soap and opened the door. He passed her in the hallway. She was wrapped up in a towel of her own but she had a different problem. He only had to cover himself from the waist down. Her towel was the same size as his and it had more ground to cover. He saw the tops of her breasts and he saw her legs clear to her thighs.

"It's all yours," she said cheerfully. "Have a nice shower, Johnny."

"Yeah," he said. "Sure."

He got under the shower and let the hot water lash at him. Hell, he thought, she was only a kid. But the trouble was that she just plain wasn't put together like a kid. Kids didn't have boobs like she did. Kids didn't have legs like that.

Maybe he should have tossed her a pass. Something easy, though, so he wouldn't scare her if she wasn't having any. It might have been worth a try.

But fourteen, for God's sake!

He said to hell with it and finished his shower.

The day was a drag. He bought himself a breakfast of waffles and bacon at the luncheonette on the corner and washed the food down with a large glass of milk. He wandered around for an hour or so but there was nothing he wanted to do and nobody he felt like running into. He didn't even have eyes to shoot pool. He was marking time, waiting for Beans to come back from his fence with money for him.

Until then there was nothing to do. He couldn't start moving without the money, couldn't even plan until he knew how much bread he would have to get started on. He shot the rest of the afternoon at a movie. There was a double feature playing at a movie house on Broadway between 88th and 89th and he hadn't seen either picture, so he went.

One was a cops-and-robbers thing called *The Mercenaries*, and the screen credits said it was based on a book that had won the Edgar, whatever the hell that meant. The other was *A Sound of Distant Drums* and it was about a group of young actors and actresses trying to get ahead in Hollywood. It bored him stiff. He sat through both pictures waiting for them to end, munching popcorn and smoking cigarettes in direct violation of fire department rules and regulations. Finally the pictures were over and he left the theater and wandered back toward 96th Street.

It was time for dinner almost, but he wasn't particularly hungry. He thought maybe he'd go down to Times Square for an hour or so and bum around down there. But he decided not to. He wanted to be around whenever Beans made the scene. He had no idea how much dough was coming to him and he was dying to find out. He wondered whether Beans would clip ten or twenty bucks off the top for himself. It was possible, and he would never find out one way or the other. But it was worth it if he did. Beans would get more than Johnny could have, even if he'd been able to find a fence willing to take a chance on him.

He checked the pool hall on the off-chance that Beans was there early. He wasn't. A guy named Phil talked Johnny into a game and they played for time—the loser picked up the tab for the games. Johnny got lucky and ran a string of six balls one time and eight the next, and from there it was easy. His eye held up and Phil wound up paying for both of them.

He left the pool hall, grabbed dinner at the luncheonette. He ate three rare hamburgers and drank a malted. His eating habits would have to change when he hit the big time, he told himself. He'd have to learn how to act in a restaurant. Not the way he'd played it last night, for example. If he was a slob, a broad might give him a fling once to see how he was in the hay. But she wouldn't want him around on a steady basis.

Hell, it was just common sense. He'd work it out. He might not be able to read a menu in French, but he'd get by. It just took a little brains, that was all.

When he got back to the pool hall Beans was there.

"Outside," Beans said. "I get nervous in the john. I'll tell you all about it."

They went outside.

They took a back booth at the candy store around the corner where the proprietor knew enough to bring them their cokes and leave them alone. Beans took a sip of his coke, lit a cigarette and smiled.

"It could have been worse," he said.

"How much?"

"I told you—it could have been worse."

"Yeah, but how much?"

Beans blew out smoke. "The watch was the big thing," he said. "The one with the suede strap, not the other one. The good one, it was an Omega."

"So?"

"Moe says it's the best watch going. A very good mechanism. Not only that but they're common. I mean, it's not like there was only one of them in the city. He can sell it easy."

"For how much?"

"How much can Moe get? I didn't ask. Retail is around three hundred. That's new, of course. This is like second-hand."

"How much did he give me?"

Beans smiled. "Ninety. That's just for the one watch. It was the big item. The table lighter, it's a Ronson and all but it isn't worth that much. Not gold just silver. The bracelet did pretty good and the engagement ring was good, diamonds like that always are. The total comes to three-ten."

"Three hundred and ten bucks?"

Beans nodded.

Johnny covered his excitement by swigging the coke. The money he had in cash plus the $310 from the stuff gave him close to five big bills.

He was rich.

It was that simple. With dough like that he could buy more clothes than he needed and take a room in a damn good hotel. There wouldn't be any more skimping, any of the hand-to-mouth routine.

Not now.

Now he was set. The money, even if he blew it in a fancier front, would last a good long while. And by the time it was gone he would have plenty coming in.

He was set.

"$310," he said reverently. "That's nice, Beans. You did good."

"That's what he gave me."

"How much do I owe you?"

Beans looked blank. "It was a favor."

"A favor is one thing. This is more."

"I just ran an errand."

"You got bread coming. A fence coulda given me thirty bucks for the watch and I wouldn'ta known the difference. How much do you want?"

Beans looked away. "I already took," he said. "I'm a rat, Johnny."

"How much did you take?"

"Twenty. You want it back you can have it. I'm sorry, Johnny. It's just—"

"You got ten more coming, man. Take it off the top and pass me the three yards."

"You mean it?"

"Course I mean it. C'mon—give me the three bills. That's plenty."

Beans made movements under the table. He separated a ten-spot from a roll and passed the roll under the table to Johnny. Johnny took it, shoved it into a pocket.

"Nobody knows about this," he said.

"I'm a clam, Johnny. You're cutting loose, aren't you?"

"Somebody say so?"

Beans shook his head. "Just a guess. The way you been acting, I don't know. Leaving the city?"

"Just the neighborhood."

"What's the bit?"

Briefly Johnny told him what he had planned. Beans listened in silence. He seemed to understand. He, too, was a professional in his chosen field of endeavor.

"Luck," he said finally. "Drop around when you get the chance. I don't know how long I'll be in town, though. It may get hot for me soon. Nobody caught me yet but people have been adding things up. The cops'll hear the rumble. They won't catch me in the act. They'll wait and jump on me when I've got a roomful of stolen stuff. I want to leave before the roof falls in."

"Luck."

Beans left the candy store. Johnny stayed where he was, ordered another coke and sipped at it. No more Beans, he thought. No more cokes. No more candy stores and no more pool halls.

Instead he'd hang out in bars and eat in posh restaurants and go to Broadway shows. There was no question about it—it would be a switch. But it would also be a change for the better, and there was no question about that either.

He laughed suddenly. He was only seventeen. Maybe the bartenders in the 59th Street bars wouldn't serve him. That would be a hell of a thing.

He laughed again.

Then he finished his coke, paid for it, and left the candy store.

He bolted his door again with the two-by-four and counted out all his money. It came to $450 and change. He was beginning to get nervous—he'd never had a roll like that before, had never even thought about that kind of bread. But he wasn't going to kick. Nobody would take the money. And in another day or two he'd be holed out in a decent hotel where you didn't have to worry about getting your money stolen.

He hid the money in the room, finding four different hiding places and dividing the money into four bundles. Then he took a subway down to Times Square and wandered around, trying his skill at a shooting gallery, grabbing a hot dog at Grant's, downing a beer in a bar on Eighth Avenue. He killed time until he was tired, then grabbed a cab back to his room and sacked out.

• • •

He woke up early. Then he stuffed his wallet with his money and went out. He skipped breakfast and took a subway down to Times Square again. He got out of the subway and kept heading downtown on Broadway. If he remembered right, there were a string of fancy men's shops from 38th Street down to Herald Square. He was right. He walked past two shops, checking the windows and getting an idea of what the styles were. Then he walked into the third he came to.

It was called Brinsley's and it was expensive. The salesman who greeted him took a good look at Johnny, starting with the dark hair cut in a d.a. and moving past the jacket to the jeans and cheap shoes. His disapproval was evident.

Johnny didn't get mad. He'd expected this. You looked like a slob and you got treated like a slob. The only way to play it was truthful—or as close to the truth as possible.

"Hello," he said. "I'm sorry about my clothes. I'm not as cheap as I look."

The salesman's jaw fell.

"I came into some money recently," Johnny said, trying to say it the way Clark Gable might have said it in a movie. "I'd like to invest in a decent wardrobe. Top to bottom. I need shoes and shirts and a suit and slacks and a jacket. I even need belts and ties and underwear. Think you can help me?"

It was the right approach. The salesman was overjoyed. He spent eight hours a day five days a week selling clothes to men who could afford them and who always bought the wrong thing. Now a good-looking young man—one who could really wear clothes—was telling the salesman to pick out a wardrobe for him. The man could not have been happier.

"Let's see," the man said. "Where should we start?"

"Any place. Everything I've got is going to go in the ashcan. So you can sell me the store if you want."

"Mind a personal question?"

"Go on."

"How much can you afford to spend?"

Johnny calculated rapidly. "Two-fifty is tops," he said. "Two hundred would be better, but I'll go two-fifty."

And they took it from there. The salesman determined Johnny's suit size and showed him half-a-dozen suits, any of which would have been fine for him.

"All values," he said. "You could spend the whole two-fifty on a suit if you wanted to. No point in it. These run from ninety to a hundred and they'd be hard to beat at any price. They'll look well and they'll hold up."

"And the style?"

"It's right," the salesman said. "On any of them. You want to look a few years older without making it obvious, don't you?"

Johnny hesitated, then nodded.

"Then take the dark gray sharkskin. You should dress conservatively. It makes sense for you anyway. You're good-looking. You don't need to have flash in your clothes. The quieter you dress, the more you stand out."

Johnny nodded. It made sense to him, and he was glad he'd levelled with the man.

"Two pairs of slacks," the man said. "Light and dark gray flannel. They'll go with the suit jacket or with the sport coat. And the best coat would be a blue blazer, I think. It's always appropriate, and if you stick with one jacket you can afford a good one. One fine jacket is better than two cheaper ones."

That's what Johnny had figured.

"And a black alligator belt," the salesman said. "Fifteen dollars and worth it. It sets a tone."

They went on and on. Underwear, two pairs of shoes, a dozen shirts.

"How about ties?"

The salesman took a breath. "Don't say I said so," he said, "but you're out of your mind if you buy ties here."

Johnny's eyebrows went up.

"Ours start at two-fifty," the man said. "Go to a tie store. Pick out nice quiet regimental stripes and don't pay more than a dollar a tie at the most. There's not a man alive who can tell the difference between a dollar tie and a ten-dollar tie."

"Really?"

"Really. And they all go in the wastebasket the minute you soil them, so the cheaper they are, the better they are. In anything else quality matters. You get what you pay for. Not ties."

They went on. The man told him that the alterations would be taken care of right away that he could pick up the clothes tomorrow. That was fine.

The salesman took out pencil and paper and carefully added a long column of figures. "That comes to $219.88 with the tax," he said. "You want to leave a deposit and pay the rest tomorrow when you pick the clothes up?"

"I'll pay it now."

"Cash or check?"

"Cash." He paid the bill and got a receipt from the salesman. Then he turned to go.

"Mr. Wells?"

Johnny turned.

"Mind a word of advice?"

"Go ahead."

"Get your hair cut."

Johnny grinned hugely liking the man very much. "I intend to," he said.

A barber used a lawnmower on his hair. When he was finished Johnny barely recognized himself. The long black hair was still black but it was no longer long. Instead he had an Ivy League cut that could have stepped right off Madison Avenue.

"You wanted it that way," the barber said.

"It's fine," Johnny told him. He tipped the barber a quarter and left.

He treated himself to a steak dinner that night, staying downtown and catching a double feature at a Times Square movie house. He didn't really want to see a movie, much less two movies, but he wanted less to hang around the neighborhood much with his hair short. People would talk. It wouldn't be good at all.

After the movie he had a glass of milk and a toasted English muffin at Bickford's. Then he grabbed a cab and went home. It was time to go to bed and he was tired.

On the way upstairs he wondered whether the landlord had gotten around to locking him out yet. He hoped not. Tomorrow he'd pick up his clothes and see about a room at a good hotel. He might as well spend the last night in the old dump, if only for old times sake.

The door was happily unlocked and he went inside, shoving his wallet between the mattress and the springs again. There was no real reason to bolt the door with the two-by-four and he didn't bother. He stretched out on the bed and let his mind make plans.

Big plans.

The salesman had been a tremendous help. He'd have gone nuts trying to pick out a wardrobe all on his own. He'd have bought all the wrong things, and he'd have wound up with junk or else have paid too much money for his clothes. This way he had all the basic essentials and they'd fit into his budget. When he got his hands on more extra cash he could always round out his wardrobe at Brinsley's. A few more jackets and some extra shirts and slacks wouldn't hurt. And another pair of good shoes might come in handy. But for now he was set.

Next came the hotel. He wasn't sure where he'd stay, but he could always worry about that in the morning. Now it was time to get some sleep. He could use it. Unless he was far off the track, the next week or so was going to be a busy one.

He got undressed, piling his clothes in a tangled heap in the corner. He'd wear them downtown tomorrow, then get rid of them for good. He got under the sheet and closed his eyes.

He was almost asleep when the door opened. His eyes fell open at once and he whirled around, ready to put up a fight to save his money.

"My God in heaven," a voice said. "You got your hair cut! You look a hundred per cent different!"

He stared. It was Linda, the fourteen-year-old. And she was wearing the same towel he'd seen her in that morning.

And nothing else.

Chapter 4

She was much prettier than he'd ever realized before. Her hair was softly blonde and she wore it in a pony tail that trailed halfway down her back. Her eyes were a very bright blue, her skin a very healthy pink. The towel was yellow, just a shade brighter than her hair. She was barefoot. He noticed that her feet were very small and daintily formed.

"I took another shower," she said. "I take a lot of showers. Especially when it gets warm. In the summer I take three or four showers a day."

He could smell the sweet after-bath smell of her. She smelled of soap and water and young beauty. He looked at her and saw how alive she was with youth. But, Christ, she was so damned young! She looked like the sister he had never had. She was young, far too young, to be in his room in the middle of the night.

"What do you want?"

She pouted. "That's not a nice way to talk, Johnny," she said. "You could at least invite me in."

"Close the door," he said.

She came in and closed the door behind herself. "Does it have a lock?"

He took a breath. "The two-by-four," he said, pointing to it.

"The hunk of wood. You jam it under the knob and it locks the door."

"I know how it works," she said. She locked the door with the two-by-four and turned to face him again.

"Now what do you want?"

"I got lonely. I thought maybe we could sit and talk for a few minutes."

"Lonely?"

"Uh-huh."

"Your old lady out?"

The girl's face darkened. "She's drunk as a pig," she said. "Every night wine. She drinks this cruddy muscatel. It's so sweet you could puke. You ever taste it?"

He shook his head. He didn't like wine.

"I had some one time. I got, you know, dragged, sort of. So I drank a few glasses of her cruddy wine. She never missed it. It tasted rotten but it made me feel all funny."

"I can imagine," he said.

"All warm," she said. "All funny inside."

He took a deep breath. "Look," he said, "I don't get it. I'm sorry I walked in on you when you were in the shower. It was a mistake. Okay?"

"Okay."

"So you can split now. I mean—"

"I know what you mean," she said. "But I want to stay."

"Linda."

Very nonchalantly she sat down on the edge of his cot, her eyes on his face. She crossed one leg over the other, and he got a momentary glimpse of the interior of her warm young thighs. He swallowed.

Easy, he told himself. You don't want this one. Tomorrow you get out, you start a new life. Complications you don't need. Fourteen-year-old girls you don't need.

"And you want me to stay," she went on.

"Like hell I do."

"Maybe you don't now," she said softly. "But you will, in a minute or two."

The towel slipped a little lower on her breasts. They showed halfway to the nipple. It seemed impossible for a girl her age to have such large breasts. They were a pale pink and they looked as firm as melons.

He tried to remember what it was like with a younger girl. Dammit he'd spent too much time with older broads. It was hard to think of what it was like with something nice and young. But Linda was just plain *too* young.

Wasn't she?

She smiled. She reached out one hand and began to stroke his chest through the sheet. The sheet was all that covered him and she stroked his chest slowly. Steady he told himself. Steady. Just relax and maybe she'll go away.

But in spite of himself he found himself responding to her. He was losing ground and she was gaining, and he knew now that it was only a matter of time. He saw the hunger building in her eyes and guessed that it was inevitable.

But such a young girl! Hell, she was a virgin, too—he was sure of it. And if there was one thing he didn't need, it was a fourteen-year-old virgin. He needed her like he needed a fractured skull.

"Nice Johnny," she cooed. "You don't know what it did to me when I was in the shower and you were in the room. I could tell you were watching me. I thought you were going to take off your clothes and come into the shower with me. I was hoping you would. I wanted you so bad that after you left I was practically shaking in the shower."

The mental picture was too exciting for words.

His opinion of her was beginning to change. If this was a virgin, he thought, then so was he. This didn't talk like a virgin or act like a virgin.

And, he went on, if she wasn't a virgin it didn't matter *how* young she was. If somebody else had already copped her, he might as well take advantage of the situation.

Why not?

"It's warm in here," she said. "I don't really need this towel any more."

And she dropped the towel.

The full sight of her bare young body was almost too much for him. Her breasts were large and they swelled outward with all the zest of full-blown youth.

His eyes followed the lines of her body. Her waist was slender, her stomach gently and perfectly rounded. Her thighs columns of pink marble.

Very nonchalantly she crossed and recrossed her legs. Once again his blood began to pound in his veins.

"You're sweating," she whispered. "I guess you don't really need that sheet at all."

And she drew the sheet from his body.

He saw the way she looked at him. This was no virgin. The eyes that studied him were not the eyes of an unexperienced girl.

Not by a long shot.

"That's better," she said. "Cooler. In fact it's *too* cool now, Johnny. Maybe we ought to huddle together for warmth. Do you think that would be all right?"

He reached for her.

She drew away, her eyes twinkling. "You're very impatient," she said. "Don't you think I ought to turn out the light?"

There were so many times when he wished the lights were off. So many women were not worth looking at, and with the lights out you had a chance to forget what they looked like.

Linda was different.

He caught her arm. "Leave the lights on," he said. "I want to look at you. I want to watch your face."

She giggled.

"And come here," he said "Now."

She came into his arms at once. She wasn't giggling any more and he knew she wouldn't be giggling until after they were done. She pressed her body to him and he held her tight.

Her skin was moist and warm from the shower. She felt unbelievably clean and she smelled marvelously sweet. He ran a hand through her silky hair, then took her face between both of his hands and kissed her.

She knew how to kiss. Her tongue crept into his mouth and she drove her body against him, pushing him down on the bed. The kiss lasted a long time. Then she leaned over him, supporting herself on her arms and gazing down into his eyes.

He reached up, took hold of her pony tail and snapped the

rubber band that held the strands of golden hair together. "To hell with this," he said. "Your hair's nice. I like it down. Loose, like. It's good like this."

She spread her hair out. It flowed over her shoulders and she looked a little older. But that didn't matter. Right now he didn't give a damn how old or young she was. He knew only that he wanted her very much.

She continued to press against him, her eyes dreamy. "Johnny," she said softly, "do you like my breasts?"

He smiled. "Nice," he said.

"You like them?"

He nodded.

"Then show me how you like them."

His hand went to her breast and cupped it gently. He didn't even move his fingers before she started to shiver. He liked the way her breast felt. It was the firmest he had ever had his hand on.

"That's nice," she purred. "They're a big pair of knobs, aren't they? I was flat as a pancake until a year ago. Then they started to sprout and they didn't stop. This last month was the real sprouting time. They grew an inch a day, I swear to God. But I think they've stopped growing by now."

"I like them this way."

"I hope they don't get any bigger."

"They're perfect now."

She smiled happily. She leaned forward. "Go ahead," she teased. "Kiss them."

He took a breast between his hands and put it to his lips. His hands went around her then, touching the smooth skin of her shoulders, moving down over her back to her buttocks.

Melons, he thought. She's a collection of melons. Melons in front, and melons behind.

His fingers moved and teased her. She wriggled, her face flushed, her eyes wild. He could see the heat building in her, could see how much she wanted it.

She raised her body, squirming crazily and small animalistic sounds came from her mouth. He nipped at her nipple with his teeth, then drew his lips away and looked at her face. Her lips were very red and she was not wearing any lipstick. Her eyes were shining, her forehead dotted with fine points of perspiration.

"You like to play games," she breathed. "I can play games too. Nice games."

He reached for her and she pulled away.

"Lie still, Johnny."

He lay still. Then she dropped on top of him again, her lips busy with his neck.

Her lips moved over his body and he grew so tense that he could barely see straight. This was fourteen years old? She acted more like an experienced waterfront prostitute than a schoolgirl. She knew more tricks than Houdini.

He was trembling.

Then she was sitting up, her hair tossed angrily over her shoulders and her breasts rampant.

"No more games," she moaned. "No more getting ready. Now, Johnny. Now!"

She rolled over and he took her. She cried out and moaned from start to finish. It did not take long—they were both too keyed-up to go on for long. It was fast and it was furious. It began and it raced forward with blinding speed, until the top was reached.

They both cried out at once into the night, cried out clearly and sharply in a single voice, cried out and were silent.

Then it was over.

Slowly, gradually, the world came back into focus. Johnny Wells lay on his back, his eyes open again now, his breathing and heartbeat back to normal. He was bathed in sweat from head to foot, sweat that was half his and half hers. He reached for a pack of cigarettes, found them, then fumbled around for matches. He shook two cigarettes loose from the pack, lit them both at once with a single match, and passed one to her.

She took it without a word, and he thought for a split-second that she wasn't really old enough to smoke, and then he remembered what they had just finished doing, and he decided that he was wrong, she was old enough to do anything in the world—and do it damn well.

He broke the silence.

"Tired?"

"A little."

"That was good, Linda. Real good."

"Uh-huh."

Suddenly he wanted to look at her. What the hell—he was never going to see her again. It would be nice to remember what she looked like.

He turned, saw her lying on her side with a warm satiated grin on her face, and he thought that maybe he *would* see her again. What the hell, he thought. He could always drop back once in a while to see what the neighborhood looked like. And he could give her the benefit of a quick fling while he was around. Sort of for old time's sake.

He leaned back, settled down again and looked at the ceiling. He flicked ashes from his cigarette to the floor. Then he remembered something he had half-seen before when he had talked to her. There had been something, but he couldn't remember what it was.

He turned on his side.

He saw the red stains.

His mind reeled. His first thought was that somehow he had hurt her. Then and only then did it dawn on him. The possibility had seemed so far-fetched that he didn't think of it for several seconds. When he did he realized it was the only explanation.

She had been a virgin.

He touched her shoulder, shook her, then pointed wordlessly. She looked and blushed.

"Why didn't you tell me?"

"I'm sorry, Johnny."

"I didn't think . . . I mean—"

"I was afraid to tell you," she said. "I was afraid you wouldn't want to with somebody who never did it before. And I thought you would be able to tell anyway once we got started. You know."

"Did it hurt much?"

"Just at first and only a little. And then everything started to get so good that I didn't care, and then it didn't hurt at all and I thought I was going to die from being so happy."

"You should have told me."

She shrugged. "I suppose so. But I was afraid you wouldn't want to do it. I mean, I'm pretty young."

"Fourteen?"

"Fourteen and two months. And you were thinking I was too young all along, weren't you?"

"Yeah."

"I could tell. So I figured I shouldn't tell you because I wanted you so bad it was hurting me and I didn't want you to kick me out. Besides, it's not like I never did anything with a boy before. I never went all the way but I came close a few times."

They lapsed into silence. He'd never been one to place much of a premium on copping a girl's honor. It was more a public service than anything else at least as far as he was concerned.

But now, surprisingly, he was strangely pleased that he had been the first with her. He didn't know exactly why he felt the way he did. It didn't make any sense, not when he added it all up and worked it out in his mind. But when all was said and done he was still glad that he had been first with her, happy that things had gone as they had.

It wasn't pride that he had seduced her. What the hell—if anything, it had been the other way around. He hadn't seduced her; she had in fact seduced him.

Still, he was pleased.

"Johnny?"

He rolled over again and dropped an arm over her. Maybe she was ready again. He wondered if she felt like a second round.

"You like me, don't you?"

"Yeah," he said. "Sure."

"Would you like it if I came to your apartment every once in a while? So we can do this again?"

He dropped a hand to her breast.

"Oh," she said happily. "Oh, I get it. You want to do it again now!"

"Yeah," he said. "Why not?"

The second time was at least as good as the first. And after it was over she rested in his arms, a smile on her face.

"I asked you a question," she said.

"I forget."

"If you'd want me to come bother you like this every once in a while. If you want for us to do this again. Or if you don't want to see me any more."

He took a deep breath. "Linda," he said, "I like you. And I like to make it with you."

She was smiling. Well, he thought, let her smile her head off. It wouldn't hurt him.

"You come over any time you want," he told her. "Any time. I'll always be glad to see you."

"I was hoping you would say that."

"I mean it."

She grinned, then got up from the bed and picked her yellow towel up from the floor. She wrapped it easily around her body.

"I better go now," she said. "Back to my own place. My mother would be teed off if I wasn't there when she woke up. She needs me so she can send me out for more wine."

He watched her as she took the two-by-four from its place, opened the door, blew him a kiss and departed. For a fourteen-year-old kid she was hell on wheels. There was no arguing about it—she was a bomb.

He bolted the door himself, then went back to bed. Sure, he thought, she could come to his room any time she wanted. What the hell did he care? Let her come. She'd get a surprise.

He wouldn't be there.

At two o'clock in the afternoon Johnny Wells walked into the Port Authority Bus Terminal on Eighth Avenue just below Times Square. He was wearing his Levi's and his leather jacket, and his Ivy cut looked wrong with them. He carried a suitcase in each hand. The suitcases were brown top-grain cowhide and they'd cost him twenty dollars each, earlier that day, in a leather goods shop on Broadway. He also carried a shoe box under each arm since the shoes hadn't fit into his suitcases.

He took the escalator to the terminal's second floor. Then he walked to the men's room. The lavatory was a very large room. It contained a row of urinals and three free public toilets. The other toilets cost ten cents. They were coin-operated.

He walked past all of them. At the back of the room there were two 25-cent booths where a person could wash and change his clothes in relative privacy. He set down his suitcases, found a quarter, and dropped it into the slot. He opened the door, hauled his suitcases and shoe boxes inside, and locked the door. Then he undressed.

He opened one suitcase and dressed himself completely in new underwear, new socks and a new shirt. He put on his gray sharkskin suit and donned one of the dozen ties he had picked up in a dollar tie store on Fifth Avenue. He dressed quickly but very carefully. Then he put on one pair of shoes and tucked the other into his suitcase. There was room for them now that he was wearing the suit.

When he was fully dressed he washed his hands and face again and dried them. Then he picked up his suitcases and left the booth, the lavatory, and the Port Authority Bus Terminal. He walked uptown to 42nd Street and waited for a cab.

Somebody was going to get a nice surprise, he thought. His clothes weren't much, but the leather jacket was in good shape. It hadn't been cheap, either. It was good leather, and in a way he was sorry to part with it. But it didn't exactly fit into the wardrobe of a Park Avenue gigolo, so to hell with it. As far as the rest of his stuff went, he couldn't see why anybody would want it.

He caught a cab quickly and loaded his suitcases into the back seat, then climbed in after them "Hotel Ruskin," he said. "That's on 37th Street."

The cabbie nodded and the taxi pulled away from the curb. Johnny had spent most of the morning checking hotels, and the Ruskin seemed like the best bet. It was a quiet residential hotel in Murray Hill, located on 37th Street between Lexington and Park. The rates seemed reasonable enough—$35 a week for a single with full hotel services and private bath. And he had enough dough to pay two weeks rent in advance.

He had talked to some flunky on the phone and the man had assured him a room was available. He hadn't made reservations, however. He wanted to see what the place looked like first.

The cab dropped him in front of a fairly impressive brick building. It had an old established air about it. The lobby was staid and conservative. The ceilings were high and the thick carpet was a subdued oriental pattern. Large copper cigarette urns filled with sand were here and there throughout the lobby.

He walked quickly to the desk, trying to look as confident as possible. The manager peered owlishly at him through a thick pair of glasses.

"I'd like to see a room," he said, speaking carefully and not slurring his words together. "Do you have a single available with a private bath?"

The man assured him that he did. He pressed a bell and a bellhop appeared from out of nowhere. He was dressed in a red uniform and was at least twenty years older than Johnny.

"Take this gentleman to 10-C," the manager said. The bellhop scooped up Johnny's bags and led him to an elevator. They left the car at the tenth floor and the bellhop led the way to a room at one end of the corridor. He opened the door with a key and motioned Johnny inside.

The room was more than adequate. The furniture was heavy and looked expensive. The bed was big. The carpet was wine-red and thick. The windows faced out on 37th Street and the view was good.

Luxury, Johnny thought. That's the ticket. We live in style from here on in.

The bellhop went around opening windows and performing other mysterious absolutions. Finally he stood at attention in front of Johnny. Johnny handed him a crisp dollar bill and watched it disappear.

"Tell him I'll be taking the room," he said. "I'll be down in a few minutes with the rent."

The man nodded and disappeared.

Johnny unpacked his suitcases, put his clothes away, some in the spacious walk-in closet and the others in the bureau. He took out a cigarette and lit it. He relaxed.

He took out the alligator billfold again and counted his money. It came to a little under $180. He'd have $110 left after he paid two weeks rent. That would be enough. In no time at all the money would start to roll in. What the hell—if a guy like Bernie could make it. he could. He had Bernie's looks and Bernie's sex appeal any day of the week.

And he had the drive.

He looked around the room. He stood up, walked to the bathroom and flushed the toilet. It flushed almost soundlessly. He looked at the tub and shower. The porcelain was spotless.

Nice, he thought. Very nice.

He undressed, took his suit and hung it neatly in the closet. He took a good leisurely shower and got out of it feeling like a new man. He dried himself on a hotel towel and drank a glass of ice-water from the ice-water tap on the sink.

Very nice.

He lit another cigarette. He sat in a chair with one leg crossed over the other and smoked. He got up, walked across the room to the window and looked out over 37th Street. He liked the view. It was better than staring at a goddamn brick wall.

Very nice.

At six o'clock he was dressed again. He left the room, took the elevator to the lobby and paid seventy dollars to the man at the desk. He walked outside. He had things to do. Dinner came first—he couldn't start work on an empty stomach. Dinner. Then work.

There was a mirror in the lobby and he stopped to study himself for a moment before he left. He barely recognized himself. The haircut changed the whole shape of his face. He looked older now, and infinitely more polished, and much more like a solid citizen. The slum-kid look was gone.

That wasn't all, he thought. Maybe they were right; maybe clothes did make the man. He looked like a million dollars now. After taxes.

It was warm out and there was a light breeze. He walked firm and easy down 37th Street with his arms swinging at his sides. He was pleased.

Nice, he thought. Very nice.

The bar was named The Vermillion Room. It was located on 59th Street across from Central Park and it was expensive. Drinks were a dollar or more.

The lighting was subdued, the carpet rich, the chairs soft and the tables small. There was no juke box. Orchestral arrangements of show tunes played continuously but unobtrusively over a well-engineered sound system. The bar itself was flat black and hyper-modern in design. The cushioned stools matched it.

Johnny Wells walked in trying to hide the fact that he was scared stiff. Act like you own the place, he thought. Walk tall. Be cool.

There were two women sitting alone at the bar toward the rear. The bartender, a portly man wearing a red cutaway jacket, was polishing a glass. The sound system played "I'll Take Manhattan".

He ignored the two women and took a stool in the middle of the bar. The barman came to him and he ordered bourbon and plain water.

He didn't want bourbon and water. What he wanted was milk, but he wasn't silly enough to order it. The bourbon came, the barman mixed the drink, and Johnny sipped it. He didn't like the taste. It was something he could put up with but he didn't care for it. Eventually he would learn about drinking. He'd find something that it was right to order and that tasted good to him. For the time being bourbon seemed safe enough.

He took a cigarette from his pack and scratched a match, dragging smoke into his lungs. That was another thing, he thought. He ought to have a cigarette case. And a lighter. Plain silver and very thin, both of them. They didn't have to cost too much to look good. But they might be important status symbols.

He smoked and sipped his drink. He listened to the music. The sound system changed to "You're The Top". He looked up and saw the barman standing in front of him.

"The one at the end," the man said. Then he moved off.

Johnny looked down at the end. The woman was about thirty-five, trying to look twenty and managing to look thirty, which wasn't too bad. She was dressed expensively and made up expensively. She was looking at him, and when he caught her eye she smiled.

That was his cue.

He picked up his drink, got up from his stool and walked toward her. Without a word he sat down on the stool next to her. He looked at her again, smiled.

She returned the smile.

"Can I buy you a drink?"

"I think so," she said. "I think you can buy me quite a few drinks."

He gestured to the bartender, indicating her empty glass with a toss of his head. The bartender came and began to prepare a rather complicated cocktail for her.

Then he felt something touch his hand. He turned his hand palm up and felt her slip a bill into it. His fingers closed around the bill. It was a ten. He paid for the drinks with it and left the change on the top of the bar. He knew there was going to be more where that had come from.

"You're a nice-looking young man," she said. "What's your name?"

"Johnny."

"Johnny," she said. "That's a nice name. I think we'll have a good time, Johnny."

Chapter 5

The salesman did not recognize the young man who walked into Brinsley's at 2:30 in the afternoon that Wednesday. He smiled his usual smile and asked if he could be of service. The young man grinned back at him.

"Don't you remember me?"

The salesman looked blank. There was something definitely familiar about the polished young man but the salesman couldn't make all the connections in his mind. He tried to cover his embarrassment.

"About two months ago," the young man said, "a fellow entered your store wearing denim trousers and a black leather jacket. You outfitted him with a complete wardrobe. Now do you remember?"

The salesman's jaw fell. He remembered now. But he didn't believe it was possible. The young hood playing Hell's Kitchen Goes To College had changed magically into a young man who could have come only from a good family, who could have gone only to an Ivy League college, who could work only on Wall Street or Madison Avenue. The transformation was astounding.

"My speech is better now," Johnny Wells said. "I use the right words and I know what they mean. And the hungry look is gone. I had a way of looking at people, adding them up, so to speak. I don't do that any more."

The salesman closed his eyes. He remembered Shaw's *Pygmalion* and his brain reeled.

"I need two more suits," Johnny Wells said. "I think a brown tweed and a dark blue Continental would be good, but any suggestions are welcome. And I can use three or four pairs of slacks and two sport jackets. Plus a pair of brown shoes and several pairs of socks and undershorts. And shirts. The striped broadcloths in the window looked rather nice."

"You've come a long way," the salesman said.

Johnny just grinned.

"How high do you want to go?"

"It doesn't really matter," Johnny said. "I want good clothes. That's all."

The salesman took a step forward. He was a little more sure of himself now. He remembered Johnny very well, remembered that he had liked the boy, and decided that he liked the present young man even more. His hand went to Johnny's tie.

"I see you still wear fifty-cent ties."

"A dollar," Johnny said. "But I thought you told me nobody can tell the difference."

"Not many people can. I'm in the trade. I have to be able to tell the difference."

Johnny sighed. "I guess you'd better sell me a dozen ties," he said.

It had been one hell of a two months.

He was sitting now in a small bar on West 47th Street between Fifth Avenue and Madison. He was alone and intended to remain alone. A small glass of cognac rested in front of him on the top of the bar.

It had taken him a few weeks to discover that cognac was the right drink for him. It tasted fine, for one thing. It was a good drink to order—dignified and not at all trite. And most important of all, the proper way to drink it was to sip it very slowly, a little at a time, with plenty of time between sips. A single drink lasted close to an hour. This was very important because he did not like to get drunk. He had become drunk once when he was trying to see whether or not he liked dry martinis. He hadn't liked them and he'd lost the fine edge of his control. He did not want that to happen again. The idea of giving up just a small portion of his self-control was galling. Cognac solved that problem for him.

He glanced at his watch, a fat gold timepiece with a stretch-link band that he'd received as a gift from a woman whose name he could not recall at the moment. It was a good watch. It looked good and kept perfect time. It told him now that it was precisely 4:27. He glanced at the wall clock over the bar and saw that the wall clock agreed with him.

In an hour he was supposed to pick up Moira for dinner. They wouldn't eat until seven or eight at the earliest, but she wanted him there at five-thirty on the dot. He decided that he would be ten or fifteen minutes late. He had discovered that it was almost a point of honor never to arrive anywhere on time.

He had upwards of half an hour to sit in the bar before it would be time to head for the hotel and change for dinner. It had taken less time to pick out clothes than he'd thought it would take. He decided to use the half hour to review the past two months. It was something he did frequently. He liked to check just where he stood and see just what it had taken to get him there.

He remembered all the way back to the first woman, the one he'd latched onto in the Vermillion Room. If she hadn't been the first she would have been easier to forget. There was nothing special about the evening—a few more drinks at the bar, then a cab ride to her apartment and a trip to bed. But she had wanted him to stay the night so that he would be around in the morning, and that was fine with him.

He couldn't sleep, so he got up and went into the living room and prowled through the bookcases. There was a large blue book on etiquette and he went through the entire book in less than four hours. This was easy enough. Most of it, he decided, was baloney. He skipped how to answer wedding invitations and what to wear to a funeral and all that sort of nonsense, but a surprising amount of information soaked into his mind and stayed there. The most important point, far more valuable than How To Shake Hands With A Duchess, was a fact which the book did not state at all but which was its underlying premise. It ran something like this—

There were two kinds of men in the world. There were gentlemen and there were bums. You were one kind or the other because there was no room in-between. You could work forty hours a week at an honest job, live in a house with wife and kiddies, and still be a bum. You could lie and cheat and steal and be a total bastard to everybody who walked into your line of vision and still be a gentleman. Neither Amy Vanderbilt nor Emily Post would have thought of phrasing it so succinctly, but there it was.

Period.

When you were a gentleman you got the right kind of attention from waiters and bartenders and salesmen and clerks. When you were a gentleman the cops gave you a wide berth. They wouldn't bug you because they knew you were out of their class. When you were a gentleman all the doors were open for you and everybody in the world was ready to accept you as an equal.

It wasn't strictly a question of money although that never hurt. You could be a millionaire ten times over and still be a bum. Or you could be a gentleman without a large roll at all, just so long as you dressed well and had a certain amount of leisure time. What made you a gentleman or a bum was less what you were than what kind of an effect you had on people. You could be a gigolo and a gentleman at the same time, because there was no contradiction in terms there.

Most of the other pretty boys who'd been in the Vermillion Room that night weren't gentlemen. They were bums, no matter how nicely they were dressed or how well they spoke. They fawned over their women and acted as a sort of cross between a butler and a puppy dog. The result was disgusting. And Johnny was fairly certain that this only cramped their style.

The next morning he made love to the woman, then had breakfast with her. He left her apartment without making any attempt for another date with her, and he didn't look in his wallet until he was back in his own room at the Ruskin.

There was a fifty dollar bill in his billfold that hadn't been there before.

The next three weeks were devoted strictly to the pursuit of the status of gentleman. For the first time in his life he became a compulsive reader. Before, a comic book or a men's magazine had been an occasional time killer at best. Now, however, he settled down to a steady routine that placed reading at the very top of the list.

He awoke every morning at nine or ten. If he was in his room at the Ruskin, as was generally the case, since most of the women wanted him to be gone when they woke up, he had a quick breakfast at the luncheonette a block away and then went directly to the main public library on Fifth Avenue and 42nd Street. If he awoke in a woman's apartment, which happened occasionally, he got away as quickly after breakfast as he could and went back to his own room to shower and shave and change clothes—then he hurried over to the library.

He never bothered with lunch. He read continuously from the time he arrived until five-thirty or six. He read everything. He concentrated at first on art and literature, racing through several general works on the subject to give himself a good background. He found out that he could remember everything of importance from what he read and that his reading speed was very high. He learned who had written what books and what in general they had to say. He found out what pictures belonged in which schools of art, and learned how to tell who had painted a certain picture. He soaked up a presentable background in these subjects in a very brief amount of time.

There was one problem. Frequently he came across words that he didn't understand. At first he would get the meaning from context, but he quickly saw that wasn't doing his vocabulary much good. Next he tried looking up each unfamiliar word as he came across it, checking meaning and pronunciation. That was a help, but it cut his reading speed to the bone and slowed him down, killing his comprehension as well. He would lose the whole thread of a paragraph or page or chapter if he had to stop and thumb through the dictionary.

He soon found the best method. He read with pen and notebook at his side, and he wrote down each unfamiliar word in the notebook without looking it up. He bought a decent dictionary which he kept in his room at the Ruskin. When he was done studying each day he went home and went through the list of new words, looking up each in turn in the dictionary and memorizing the word and its spelling and pronunciation. He tried using each word in a sentence so that it would become a part of his vocabulary. That procedure worked best for him. At first the word lists for each day were very long. Gradually they became shorter and his vocabulary increased at a rapid pace.

Gradually his reading interests spread to cover wider and wider areas. He raced through a basic text on Grecian civilization, another on the Roman world. This led him in two directions. He pored over two books on other ancient civilizations and several on medieval and Renaissance history and culture. He found other books on more contemporary history, working his way right up to the present time.

The more he learned, the more he found himself not knowing. A short history of colonial America made him realize that he had to know some economics in order to understand what he was reading about, and he burned his way through two fundamental economics texts and got the knowledge he wanted. Another history book led him into sociology.

The sociological jargon was almost impenetrable until he discovered Thorstein Veblen and read all of Veblen in three days.

The style was hard until he got used to it. Then it read quickly and he soaked up more theories and doctrines.

At the same time he realized that he was learning in a vacuum. He took to checking through the *Times* every morning with his breakfast until he had a pretty good idea of what was going on in the world. This helped round him out. It gave him a better picture of what people were doing, of what was happening, and his mental image of a gentleman was taking more solid shape.

That's how he spent his days. His nights, of course, were used to different purpose—that of survival. He stuck with 59th Street for a week, then switched his hunting grounds east to Lexington Avenue in the Fifties. The women there seemed to have more polish and just as much money.

He made the scene at the bars four and sometimes five times a week. There were occasions when no woman seemed interested in him, but those occasions were relatively few and far between. His appearance certainly didn't hurt him, and neither, he was pleased to discover, did his increasing ability to converse intelligently. The women were not disappointed to find a young man who could find a more stimulating topic of discourse than clothes and food and sex.

When he went looking for a woman he usually wound up with her at her apartment, or at a hotel which she chose. Once or twice the woman had insisted upon coming up to his apartment, which annoyed him. But the room was more than presentable and the hotel staff did not seem to object if he brought a woman to his room. He was an ideal tenant. He paid his rent before it was due, kept his room immaculate, and never was drunk or disorderly.

And the women he brought with him always behaved themselves. They were not tramps.

Some of the women had unusual tastes. One, whom he had been with twice, did not want him sexually at all. She was content to sit and talk with him, or merely to have him around. Her kick, he discovered, was simply to be seen in the company of a good-looking and intelligent young man. On their second date, which she had arranged over the telephone, he was only required to escort her to and from a party in a plush suite at a Park Avenue hotel. At the party he acted not like a domesticated gigolo but like a human being, which was what the woman wanted. He mingled with the other people there, used his newly-acquired knowledge in several enjoyable conversations, and enjoyed himself tremendously.

Another woman liked to be skillfully and painstakingly seduced. Another was virtually insatiable and left him totally exhausted—he made love to her a staggering total of six times in a single night and felt that he had more than earned the hundred dollars she gave him. Such women he very carefully avoided in the future.

There was one thing he had not done. He had not made anything resembling a permanent connection with a woman. Several of them knew his address and could call him on the phone if they wanted him for one reason or another, but no single woman was keeping him.

He had received an offer or two, vague ones that he could and did pass up easily. He both wanted and didn't want a permanent alliance. It was security, and more money generally, and a better introduction into the world of the gentleman. But something inside him made him pass up those offers that he'd had. He wasn't sure what it was.

Sometimes he thought that he was waiting for a better opportunity—either a proposal of marriage or a permanent association with a woman who was very rich and, at the same time, somewhat desirable. On other occasions he thought that he was simply resisting the notion of being tied to one woman, living with her constantly and being always at her beck and call. As what he privately termed a freelance gigolo he retained a good measure of his independence. He wasn't sure that he wanted to relinquish it.

There was one other possibility that occurred to him from time to time. In two months he had come one hell of a long way from a one-room roach trap on 99th Street. He had changed both his way of life and his personality as well. From a two-bit punk without a pot he had metamorphosed into an intelligent young man with a savings and checking account. It only stood to reason that this process of change would continue. If he had come so far in two months, he would probably change still more in the following two months. There was no way to tell what sort of person he would become.

And as far as he could see he would be tying himself off if he hooked up with a woman on a steady basis. He'd be putting himself in a backwater trading his potential for growth in exchange for a form of security which he did not really need. It wouldn't hurt him to wait. He was young enough to bide his time and see what was going to happen to him.

His watch told him it was five minutes past five when he downed the last drop of his cognac and put a bill on the bar top for the barman. He left the bar and caught a taxi back to his hotel.

It was time to shower and shave and dress. Then it would be time to see Moira.

Moira Hastings was something a little bit special.

She was thirty, which made her young by comparison with the other women who were Johnny's usual clients. She was also quite attractive. Her appeal was less the Hollywood image of beauty than the *Vogue* image of chic sophistication. She was tall for a woman and she was very slender, with firm, pointed breasts and very slight hips. Her hair, originally a rather mousey brown, was dyed a pleasant rust shade. She wore it in a French roll and did not let it down when she made love, which she did quite well.

Any number of men would have been more than willing to keep her company and join her in bed for no remuneration whatsoever. She was not the type of woman who needed a paid lover, and Johnny would not have been able to figure her out if he hadn't boned up on some elementary Freudian psychology. Now, however, he knew pretty well what made her tick.

She was a modern woman in the full sense of the word. She had graduated *magna cum laude* from Vassar and had taken graduate work at a school of interior design. After distinguishing herself at that school she found a well-paying job with a top firm of interior decorators. She stayed with the firm until her contacts were established in the field and then struck out on her own. Now she was a leader in her profession. Her income was sky-high and her work ideal.

Moira had been married once, and briefly, to a man named Gerald Raines. He was a Wall Street investment counsellor and came from a wealthy and well-established Philadelphia Main Line family. She divorced him after less than a year, obtaining a Nevada decree on grounds of extreme mental cruelty. The divorce went uncontested. She asked no alimony and no settlement. She wanted only her freedom.

That, Johnny knew, was the whole story of Moira Hastings. She was a career woman to the core. She wanted to call the shots and she did not want to be tied to anybody or anything. This made her the type of woman who preferred a paid companion to a voluntary one, if only *because* she paid for what she got. The money she spent established her relationship to her lover beyond any shadow of doubt. She was in the driver's seat, now and forever. Her lover was not her equal and was not designed to be her equal. In this respect she was not dissimilar to a man who preferred a mistress or a whore to a wife.

She was not bossy and she was not demanding. She made certain that her superiority was recognized but she never became obnoxious about it. She was generous—her orientation made her lover the more desirable as his cost to her increased. She never gave Johnny presents, as many women did. Only money.

Johnny liked her.

He called for her at twenty minutes of six. Her apartment was on 53rd Street near Park Avenue. She occupied the entire second floor of a reconditioned brownstone and, naturally, she had decorated it herself. The decor was a little modern for Johnny's taste but he had to admit that she'd done a hell of a good job with the place.

She was ready for him and she looked lovely. There was a fragile look about her, as if a man might crush her if he held her too tightly in his arms. Johnny closed the door and she came to him, her face up to be kissed. He held her gently and kissed her on the mouth.

"Sorry I'm late," he said. "I was reading and I didn't notice the time."

"That's all right."

They walked together into the living room. He went to the bar, took gin and vermouth and made them into a martini for her. He poured himself a very small drink of cognac and they sat together on the couch and sipped their drinks in silence.

"Hell of a day," she said finally. "That bitch of a Sutter woman has the taste of a barbarian. I showed her the color scheme for her damned house and she screamed. You should have seen what she wanted me to do to the place. Her idea of decoration is a cross between Byzantine and Mayan stupidity with a little jungle stupidity included. I think I managed to talk her out of it."

He said something appropriate.

"You should see the house," she told him. "She must have driven the architect out of his mind. Try to imagine a cross between Frank Lloyd Wright and a Romanesque cathedral."

He did, and shuddered.

"Uh-huh. That's the idea. I got the story on how she wound up with the house, too. She hired Jacob Rattsler to do it. He's as good a man as you can find and his price is high. He's generally worth it. Then she explained just what she wanted and Jake's stomach turned over a few times."

"I can understand why."

"You only think you can. You never saw the house. Hell, you

never met the woman, Johnny. He told her he'd give her just what she wanted but he refused to take credit for the house. He wouldn't sign his name to the sketches. She was dumb enough to go along with it and Jake decided to make it just as rotten as it ought to be for her to live in it. He may have had a little fun, because he came up with the most incredible monstrosity in all of upper Westchester. And she loves it. She thinks it has character."

"Why don't you give her the same treatment?"

"I'd love to. I'd really love it." She sighed and took out a cigarette, put it to her lips. Johnny lit it for her. "But Jake can afford something like that. He's got a reputation for eccentricity anyway and he's established at the top. I'm not that outstanding yet. And interior decorators aren't supposed to be oddballs. They're supposed to be sincere professional craftsmen, not nuts."

She tossed off the rest of the martini and put the glass on the coffee table. "To hell with Martha Sutter," she said. "Let's get some food, Johnny. Where would you like to eat?"

He pretended to think about it, then played the game the way it was supposed to be played. "Anywhere," he said. "I'll leave it up to you."

She always asked him where he wanted to eat. He always let her choose the spot. It was a little ceremony they went through, and he felt it was quite consistent with the rest of her personality. She wanted him to leave the decisions to her, and at the same time they had to pretend that he was doing this because he didn't care one way or the other.

They wound up at La Tete de Nuite, an expensive French restaurant in the east Sixties. Provencal murals decorated the walls and the waitresses wore abbreviated *gamine* costumes that stayed in good taste while revealing as much as possible of the girls, whose charms were definitely worth revealing.

The menu was entirely in French, which didn't bother Johnny at all. He read it easily and ordered a shrimp cocktail, onion soup, and duck with orange sauce.

This was the result of another facet of his studying. Most evenings before he went to make the rounds of the pick-up bars he found a good restaurant which he'd never been to before. He had no more shame there over his ignorance than he had had at Brinsley's with the clothing salesman. He asked the waiter the name of each entree, what it was, how it was pronounced. By now he could read menus in French, Spanish, German and Italian. He knew what each dish was and what it tasted like and how to order it—and he knew what wines went with what food.

Moira ordered lobster thermidor and he selected a dry Chablis to go with their meal.

The meal was excellent. While they ate their chocolate eclairs and drank their steaming demitasse, Moira passed him a twenty under the table. He paid the waiter, left a good tip and pocketed the change. This, too, was standard operating procedure. He would just as happily have paid the tab himself, since he was able to afford it and knew he would get the money back from her. But she liked to pass him the money; it was another barely subtle reminder of their relationship. By giving him money she reinforced her position in the affair.

They left the restaurant and taxied back to her apartment. He put his arm around her in the back seat of the cab and she relaxed against him. He guessed that she would want to make love when they were inside the apartment. White wine almost always had an aphrodisiacal effect upon women.

He was right.

"Kiss me," she said. He took her in his arms. She was tall but not as tall as he was, and she stood on the tips of her toes, pressing her mouth to his. Her mouth opened quickly and his tongue shot into it. Her mouth was warm, sweet from the wine and as he kissed her she ground her hips gently but sensually into his.

Now we switch, he thought.

That was more of the pattern. As soon as their relationship turned sexual their roles were reversed. He was supposed to be the aggressive male, she the submissive eternal female. It was an obvious reversal—he was not supposed to be the cave man, batting his mate over the head and dragging her off to his lair by her hair. Not quite.

Instead he took her and led her to the couch, where he kissed her some more and began the preliminary fondling of her breasts. She lay relatively passive in his arms, enjoying his kisses and caresses, and he told her how beautiful she was, how fine she was. The words came automatically from his lips and he wondered whether she heard them or whether they served solely as a kind of verbal background music for their activity. A little of both, he decided. A little of both.

Finally he raised her in his arms, stood up and carried her to the bedroom, stopping to kiss her passionately on the way. He was glad that she wasn't heavy—as it was, it wasn't much trouble at all to carry her to the bedroom. But some of the women he'd had would have given him a hernia.

He set her down in the bedroom and closed the door. Then

they went into the next part of their ritual. She raised her arms high over her head and stood as motionless as a statue. She closed her eyes.

He stood before her. Briefly he ran his hands over her body. His hands lingered at her breasts and buttocks. She had large breasts, firm and pointed, but her buttocks were taut without an ounce of extra flesh.

Then he dropped his hands. For a moment he, too, stood motionless. Then he began to undress her.

He pulled the dress slowly over her head and folded it over the arm of a chair. He removed her half-slip, her bra, her garter belt and stockings, her panties. When he took off her shoes and stockings and panties she stood poised on first one foot and then the other, so that he could get the clothing off. When she was naked he stood and looked at her, then removed his own clothing as well.

Then he moved close to her again and began to caress her nude body. His hands took hold of her breasts and squeezed gently. He touched her thighs. He kissed her throat.

C'mon, he thought. Get going. It's your cue.

She knew her cue. Her eyes opened and she gave a little sigh as she fell into his arms. She pressed her mouth to his while her hands amused themselves. She began to breathe very hard and very fast all at once, and he bent over to scoop her up easily in his arms and deposit her gently on top of the bed. He held her with one hand while he pushed the covers away. Then he laid her down and stretched out beside her.

There was one good thing, he thought. The ritual was pure baloney phony from start to finish, but it had one definite point in its favor. For some odd reason the little game the two of them played made him responsive as a Texas longhorn. The simple act of undressing her while she stood like a statue got him excited. He didn't need to work at it.

He took her breast to his lips and kissed hard. He ran his hand down over her flat stomach. She was all smooth and clean and she smelled of a pleasantly subtle perfume. He fondled her to heighten the flow of excitement that was coursing through her.

At first, he thought, he'd been a little in awe of Moira. More than a little. She was a new type of woman for him, something a little bit special, and he'd been fascinated by her.

That was changed now.

She was still exciting, but now he could see through her and that changed a lot of things. When you could see the uncertainty and foolishness in a woman you couldn't set too great a prize on her. She had clay feet just like all the other statues. She was more fun than most, but she was still just a client, just a field to be plowed.

Now it was time to plow.

Hang on, he thought. This one will knock your hat off.

And then it began. She was violently excited now and she wasn't making any attempt to contain the fury of her passion. Her nails raked his back and her teeth were active on his shoulder

And then things began to happen faster and faster, and she thrashed violently on the expensive bed, and even the expensive bed groaned in metallic protest at the fury of their violent love-making.

Faster.

The world began to dip and sway, and the dominant woman

submitted to violent male activity, and he was on top now, he was the boss, he was the king, and it was happening, happening.

They crested and the whole world went crazy.

They were sitting up in bed, smoking cigarettes and reading. He was reading a copy of *Partisan Review*. She was leafing through *House Beautiful* and making sarcastic comments.

Suddenly she put down the magazine.

"I can't take it," she said. "The pace. I'm going to tell that Sutter bitch to cool her heels for a while. I'm going to get out of this damned town for a week. No, make that two weeks."

"Where are you going?"

"On a vacation," she said. "I don't know where. Vegas, maybe. I was there once for a weekend. I got my divorce in Reno but I drove to Vegas once. It's a good town. You throw your money away and relax and enjoy it."

He didn't say anything.

"Two weeks," she said. "And maybe I'll run it to three if I feel like it. Ever been there?"

He shook his head.

"Want to come along?"

Chapter 6

He played it cool but not too cool. He knew that if he acted as enthusiastic as he felt he'd be weakening his position. She valued articles in accordance with her difficulty in obtaining them. So he played hard to get—but not too hard.

"I don't know," he said. "It's a distance."

"Travel is broadening. You must be getting sick of this town, Johnny."

"It's a good town. I don't know."

"Think about it."

He thought, or pretended to. "How would we work it? I don't care for artificial husband-and-wife routines."

"Adjoining rooms. A good hotel asks no questions. Especially in Nevada."

He nodded. "That seems sensible," he said. "But why would you want me along?"

"For company. You know me, Johnny. I get lonely easily. And I enjoy your company."

He didn't put up much of an argument but let himself be talked into it easily from that point on. The arrangements were simple enough. She would pay all expenses—air transportation there and back, the hotel bill, all meals. She'd give him spending money and gambling money.

It sounded fine.

The next morning he paid two more weeks rent on his room at the Ruskin, told the manager he'd be out of town for an indeterminate period of time, and packed his two suitcases. He didn't want to check out of the Ruskin, not for two weeks rent. He liked the room and wanted it to be waiting for him when he returned. Besides, he couldn't take all his clothes with him. He had to have a place to leave them.

He met Moira and they taxied to LaGuardia, caught a flight to Vegas non-stop. They registered in adjoining singles at the Calypso House, the newest and most expensive hotel and gambling palace on the Strip. They went to their rooms, changed, and met in the hallway. Johnny figured they'd grab a bite to eat, then see a show or something. But he hadn't figured out Moira's second greatest vice, second only to sex.

It was gambling.

They went to the casino right off the bat and she bee-lined for the roulette wheel, pausing only to convert a thousand dollars into fifty-dollar chips. He followed her and stood by her side. She bet the chips one at a time, betting an individual number on each spin of the wheel. He watched her lose two hundred fifty dollars in five straight spins of the wheel. It was her money, but he couldn't figure out why she wanted to throw it away on sucker bets. The house had the percentage no matter what kind of gambling you were doing. Otherwise there wouldn't be any house. But the house edge in roulette was a little better than average, which was frightening. Not as bad as the horse races, maybe, but bad enough.

"Why don't you switch to craps," he suggested. "The odds are better."

She turned on him. She handed him four chips. "You switch to craps," she said.

"I didn't mean—"

"I'd rather play alone," she snapped. "Meet me later."

He didn't argue with her. He took the chips and held them in the palm of his hand. Fifty bucks a chip, he thought. He could put all four on one roll of the dice if he wanted. He could bet them one at a time. Or he could cash them in, tell her he'd lost his money. It wouldn't matter whether she believed him or not, because she wouldn't give a damn.

He compromised. He walked to the nearest cashier's cage and passed over the four chips. "Cash two of these," he said. "And break the rest into dollars."

The cashier did a long double take and Johnny decided that it must have been an unusual request. It made sense to him. He'd drag half the money for himself, then use the others to pass the time. Gambling wasn't his kick, but it would make the time pass a little faster.

The cashier followed instructions. Johnny put two fifties in his wallet and found his way to a crap table. He played the way very few people play dice. He bet only against the shooter and made his bets only after the shooter had rolled his point. When it was his turn with the dice he passed. His bet was always two dollars, never more and never less.

When you shoot craps in this manner the odds are slightly in your favor. If you do it long enough, and consistently enough, you will get rich. If you do *anything* long enough and consistently enough with the odds always constant and unyielding in your favor, you will grow rich.

This is mathematics.

He played for two hours. He passed the dice many times in the course of the two hours, a practice which seemed to amuse some of the players. They couldn't understand why he didn't want to roll.

He was even with them. He couldn't understand why they'd buck the odds.

At the end of the two hours he cashed in one hundred and forty dollars worth of chips. It was a small profit but it pleased him. He had been lucky. The odds weren't that strongly in his favor. At one point, when a shooter made five straight passes, he was beginning to lose faith in higher mathematics. But he was pleased.

He wandered back to the roulette wheel. Moira wasn't there. He looked around, spotted her at another cashier's cage. She was buying more chips. He wondered whether this was her second trip to the cage—or her twentieth.

He never found out. She didn't talk about how much she lost, and he knew better than to ask her. If she wanted him to know she would tell him herself.

She was a creature of patterns, and once again the pattern was established and followed to the letter. Every day she gave him two hundred dollars when they finished breakfast at noon or later. They met for dinner—then she returned to the casino and he amused himself whatever way he wanted. At night he made love to her if she indicated that she was in the mood. She did so rarely, never two nights in a row and never more than one time in one night.

He had enough time for himself so that he could line up women on his own. Money didn't bother him—he was making a minimum of a hundred dollars a day from Moira—so he no longer spent his time looking for wealthy women ready to pay for him. Instead he shopped for what he wanted.

He picked up a waitress in a restaurant and spent a hectic evening at her cottage. She was young and blonde and wild. Sex was her sole interest and she couldn't get enough to make her happy. While they rested between bouts she told him anecdotes of her own personal and none-too-private life.

"One time I did it with five boys at once," she said happily. "Can you imagine?"

He couldn't imagine.

"Five at once," she repeated dreamily. "You never felt anything like it. Groovy."

"You mean one after the other?"

"No, all at once, dummy. I did it like one after the other lots of times. You know, like a line-up. More than five, you can bet on it. Sixteen one time. One after the other, sixteen of them, I like to die it felt so good. But this time the five was at once, all of them."

He asked her how she had managed it.

"One here," she explained. "Naturally. And another one there. That much they call a sandwich. Then another one here and two more here and there. See?"

He saw.

"It's too bad there weren't two more guys," she added. "I still had two hands free. But the hell with it. Let's go again, Johnny."

Fortunately for his health, the one evening was all he spent with the nymphomaniacal waitress. But despite such distractions he still spent a great deal of time thinking about Moira. She wasn't even gambling sensibly. She reversed the usual gambler's desperation play—whenever she won a bet she kept doubling up until she lost it all.

It was a simple case of her constantly trying to lose everything she had.

He tried to fit that in with what he knew about her. She wanted to be independent, wanted to be on top with no strings attached. And at the same time she felt that she was bad, and she was losing her money at the roulette wheel because she wanted to punish herself. That much almost anybody could figure out, he thought. But he would never know why.

Not that he cared. He was making good money doing next to nothing. He was getting rich, and in another couple of days they'd be on their way back to New York and he'd have a roll of dough to stash in the bank. If she wanted to be an idiot that was her business. He didn't give a damn. He was making his profit and the hell with her.

There was only one thing he'd been worried about when she suggested the trip. The feeling persisted that some other guy might beat his time with her and he'd be out in the cold. But that didn't bother him now. Vegas was swimming with pretty boys who could be made for a price—some of them ready to roll with a man or a woman, whoever asked first. But Moira was barely interested in him, let alone anybody else. The gigolos patently ignored her. They knew well enough that she wasn't having any. Johnny had no worries.

At least he thought so.

It was Saturday night. It had been a pretty ordinary day for Johnny—breakfast at one in the afternoon, a swim in the hotel pool, an hour at the crap table during which he'd dropped seventeen dollars, dinner with Moira, a floor show at another hotel down the Strip. He'd gone to the show alone—Moira was too busy losing money to be bothered with entertainment. He felt like pointing out that she could spend as much money on the floorshow as she could lose, but didn't bother. He figured that she might fail to appreciate his wit.

He walked into the lobby of the Calypso House, got his key at the desk and rode upstairs in the elevator. Moira would be downstairs in the casino, he guessed. She seldom quit before two-thirty and it was only a few minutes past one.

When he saw her door ajar he thought her apartment was being frisked. But that didn't seem logical—what burglar left the door ajar and turned the light on? None he had ever heard of.

His next thought was that she was in her apartment and letting him know that she wanted him. But that didn't seem too logical either. That wasn't the way she went about things. It didn't make any sense.

The third thought, at last, made sense. Moira or a maid had left the door open and the light on by mistake. He decided to kill the light and shut the door.

He opened the door a few more inches so that he could reach the light switch.

Then he saw them.

And froze.

There was sight, and there was recognition, and then there was disbelief. His eyes stared blankly ahead as he watched a scene that made no sense to him at all.

He could have reacted in either of two ways. He could have backed away, very quietly, possibly drawing the door shut as he did so.

Or he could have charged into the room, raising hell as he did so, and causing quite a stir.

He did neither of these things.

Instead he stood right where he was and watched. He couldn't believe what he was seeing but he went right on watching anyhow. It was a new one on him. He held his breath for several seconds, then let it out.

And went right on staring. This is what he saw:

A girl with red hair lay on her back in the center of the bed. Her eyes were closed, her mouth open. She was breathing raggedly. From time to time her body gave a twist of pleasant excitement.

Another person crouched over her. The other person was kissing her breast now while fondling Moira elsewhere.

The other person was a girl.

A very pretty girl. A girl with short black hair and tiny rosebud breasts. A girl with mannish hips.

A girl.

Johnny was staggered. He went on watching as the girl began planting a row of kisses on Moira's body just as he himself had done so many times, to Moira and to many other women. It was normal for a man to kiss a woman like that. But when a girl did that it wasn't normal at all. It was sick and twisted.

It was also happening before his eyes.

The girl kissed lower.

She took a long time finding what she was looking for, and all the while Moira's excitement grew visibly.

And then, amazingly, the brunette was reversing her position on the bed. And then Moira did something Johnny didn't believe. She drew the girl down to her.

Johnny gasped.

And Moira duplicated the actions of the brunette. They went on and on and on.

I wish I had a camera, Johnny thought.

He sighed. One of those precious moments preserved and immortalized on film would be a damned annuity. Moira had said that interior decorators weren't supposed to be eccentric, hadn't she?

Well, this was eccentric enough. And she would pay through the nose until the day she died to keep that kind of picture out of circulation.

Because this was a pretty eccentric taste. And taste was precisely the word for it.

They kept kissing, and Johnny was going out of his mind. Maybe it was never going to end, he thought. Maybe they would just plain go on forever. It was crazy, and it was strangely terrifying and it was sickening. But it was sure as hell happening, and there was no way of getting around it.

In a way, he thought, it explained a lot of things. Moira wanted to be independent from men, and at the same time she needed a lot of sex. So she bought her men and stayed independent that way. But that wasn't enough.

There was only one real way to stay independent from men. It was simple enough. You gave up men and tried women instead. And that was just what she was doing.

It seemed to be working.

Johnny felt like a fifth wheel. More than that, he felt like a third wheel on a two-wheel bicycle. He wanted to leave but couldn't.

Then, finally, they were done. They fell apart, exhausted, and Johnny slipped away from the door without being seen, closing it a few inches first so that no one else could look in. He went to his own room next door, took out his key and went inside. He felt sick to his stomach.

Moira didn't want him again. She barely wanted him around at all, and it wasn't hard for Johnny to figure out why. She and the brunette were together almost constantly. They gambled together, but now Moira wasn't throwing her money away quite so recklessly. They ate together and they drank together. They went to shows together. Johnny Wells was left out in the cold, and that suited him fine.

He didn't want to have anything to do with her if he could help it. He didn't even want to ride back to New York with her. She didn't want him and he didn't want her and to hell with it.

So he went to her.

"I think I'll go back a day early," he said. "If it's okay with you."

"Do what you like," she said. "I may stick around an extra week. I'm having a ball, even if I am taking a licking."

She certainly picked the right words, he thought.

"Well," he said, "how about my ticket?"

"I bought one-way tickets."

"Want to give me money, then?"

"Buy your own ticket," she snapped. "I'll take care of your bill and that's all. You've milked me for enough dough already, sonny boy. From here on you can fend for yourself."

It was a complete switch. He could have put up a fight but he didn't even bother. The plane fare would set him back less than two hundred bucks and it was worth it to him to avoid an argument. She'd changed from an independent woman who paid for her men to a militant dyke who didn't want anything to do with them. Well, the hell with her.

He packed and caught a plane that landed at Idlewild. He went back to his room at the Ruskin and deposited a pile of dough when his bank opened the next morning. He was free now, out on his own hook again. He decided to stick with freelancing. A permanent hook-up was a pain in the neck even for two weeks. He tried to imagine living with a broad like Moira for a year. Or one who was worse, for that matter. It would be hell on earth and who needed it?

For two weeks he didn't go near a woman. It was a tremendous switch for him, a brand-new approach to the whole concept of a vacation. He lived at the Ruskin, went to concerts and shows, sat in the park and read books. He wandered around the city and stayed away from the bars on Lexington.

What the hell, he could afford it. He had more money than he could spend for a while and he didn't need to bang his head off to get his hands on more. He wasn't the kind of man who went through money like a fish out of water anyhow. He spent a lot certainly, but that was because he earned a lot. His expenditures were never as high as his income.

He wasn't a compulsive spender or a compulsive gambler. And he deserved a vacation. So for those two weeks he ate well, took life easy, did a lot of loafing and a lot of wandering. It was a kick.

He thought quite a bit about Moira during those two weeks. Sometimes he had to laugh. He would look at the whole situation objectively and it would seem hysterically funny to him. The whole idea of a woman paying a guy to be on hand to make love to her and then taking up with a dyke was a pretty hilarious notion. You had to laugh when you thought about it. What the hell—it was funny.

Other times it wasn't so funny.

Because during those other times he would think that Moira had taken up with the dark-haired dyke because the girl made love better than he did. That was ridiculous, of course—Moira's problem was psychological, not physical. He could have been Adonis himself and she still would have shown a preference sooner or later for the girl's style of lovemaking.

So it wasn't his fault. But still it was galling. He was something of an expert in his field. One session with him ought to turn a devout lesbian into a heterosexual. Instead it had worked the other way around and it was annoying. He had trouble thinking about it without getting more than a trifle angry.

He had the weird feeling that he was coming to some sort of a division in the road. That was one reason he had taken the vacation, such as it was. He wanted to leave himself some good thinking time. He had to be able to see where he was and what the hell he was going to do next.

Where was he?

In a sense he was rich. His two bank accounts totaled almost seven thousand dollars—which was pretty damned high by 99th Street standards. Yet you could look at it another way. Moira probably dropped more than that in a bad day at the roulette wheel. So he wasn't so rich after all.

Well, what did he want? He'd already managed to learn that he didn't want a permanent hook-up with a woman. That would only drive him nuts. Nor did he want to keep freelancing, socking more and more money away, until he was rich. What would he do then? Sit around and rot?

There were moments and even hours when he envied the suckers with their nice steady jobs. They had something to do every day, something that interested them, while he had nothing but time on his hands and no real future.

The rest of the time he gave himself mental kicks in the head and asked himself if he was out of his mind or what. He had money to burn, easy work and simple hours. What was wrong with him? Did he want to tie a ball and chain around his neck?

To hell with it, he thought. He'd just keep on the way he was. He was doing a lot of reading, seeing shows, eating well. He was making money. Hell, he was enjoying himself, wasn't he? Of course he was. So why kick a winner in the head?

Maybe I've been reading too much, he thought. Maybe I'm getting a little bit nuts. Maybe the philosophy and psychology and history and literature is too much for my head to take. Maybe I'm looking around corners for little men who aren't there.

He talked to himself like that but it didn't work. Not quite.

Because the nagging feeling persisted that he was missing

something that was necessary to the full enjoyment of life. He couldn't help feeling that there was a vacuum-like quality to his life as it stood and he didn't know what the hell was the matter with him. It was a pain in the neck, he thought angrily. If you just got to feeling rotten when you were a success, what was the point in trying at all?

There were even times when he remembered the days of poverty on the upper west side with something approaching nostalgia. Then he would think about cockroaches and cramped filthy quarters and not enough to eat and he would realize that the good old days hadn't been so good at all.

Then why did they seem good?

Maybe I was alive then, he would think. Maybe I was more of a human being and less of a machine. But was I a human being then? I never read a book or thought a human thought. I didn't *live* like a human being. I lived like an animal. Was I actually more human then?

It didn't make sense.

Nothing made sense.

If there was only a way to turn your mind off, he thought. To just plain close your eyes tight and not think about anything at all. Maybe that would be the best bet. But it had taken him a hell of a long time to learn how to think.

How did he learn to stop thinking?

It was confusing as all hell.

He went back to work on a Wednesday evening. He had dinner alone, then dressed in his brown tweed suit, white shirt with tab collar, brown foulard tie, and Scotch grain brown loafers. He told a cab driver to take him to Lexington and 58th Street and walked into the Pickled Poodle feeling like a prostitute at the conclusion of her period.

Back to work.

Two hours and forty-three minutes later he was in bed with a forty-year-old woman named Margaret Pennington who had a husband, but the husband was out of town and Mrs. Pennington was consequently *on* the town. They made a rather dispirited sort of love in Mrs. Pennington's nuptial chamber and, while Mrs. Pennington seemed to be going out of her mind over the way things were proceeding, Johnny couldn't have cared less. It was a complete bore from start to finish, and he made sure the finish came as quickly as possible.

An hour later she wanted to play games again.

The thought kind of nauseated him but he wanted to give her her money's worth. What the hell, she was paying for it.

But something was going wrong.

She was getting excited, all right. If she got much more excited she would go through the roof, which would be fine. But he wasn't getting excited.

The spirit was willing. But the flesh wasn't.

This was something which had never happened before. There had been many times when he'd had no interest in making love. There had been many times when he had not enjoyed the process in the least for one reason or another, either because the woman was unappealing or because he was tired or because the woman was about as much fun as a sweaty pillow. This was something else.

Something brand new.

It didn't take long for him to realize that nothing was going to happen. His first reaction was simple enough. He had to cover himself.

"Margaret," he said, tender as all hell, "I don't think I'll be able to make love to you a second time tonight."

This displeased her.

"I certainly want to," he lied. "I want to very much. But I'm afraid I can't. You see—" he grinned sadly "— you really tired me out. I guess I'm not used to women like you, Margaret. You're a lot of woman."

This was the most phenomenal misstatement of recorded time but it worked magnificently. Since nobody had told Mrs. Pennington she was a lot of woman since the opening of the Panama Canal, she was more pleased than she would have been if he had taken her an even dozen times. She told him at least fourteen times to think nothing of it, it couldn't be helped, and at any rate their one experience was more than satisfactory.

To hell with you, he thought. You probably haven't done it twice in one night since they shot Lincoln. So you've got nothing to gripe about.

When he left she gave him one hundred and seventy-two dollars, which struck him as an unlikely sum but certainly more than sufficient. He was pleased by the payment but roundly disturbed by his own performance, or lack thereof. Despite what he'd said to old Margaret, she hadn't taken anything out of him but desire. Making love to any woman twice in one night was nothing for him. And to top it off, he hadn't had *any* woman in better than two weeks.

So what was wrong?

It happened again the night after that. This was worse, because it happened the *first* time and he certainly couldn't plead exhaustion. Nor could he rationalize his failure to himself. The woman involved was not unappealing by a long shot. She was a neat little number cheating on her husband and she had a body that couldn't have been better.

But nothing happened.

Again he covered himself, this time in a different way. "Darling," he warbled, "you must get bored with the usual run of lovemaking. I want to make love to you in a new and different way."

She was all for it. She said something properly silly about variety being the spice of life and he gave her enough spice to fill a few hundred pepper mills. He satisfied her skillfully without revealing his impotence.

This may have satisfied her but it sure as hell didn't satisfy him. It kept him from sleeping that night. He tossed and turned in his own bed all night long, and when he finally did drift off to a hazy sort of sleep it was beset by continual nightmares. He woke up exhausted, feeling as though he'd just finished running twenty miles with an eighty-pound albatross around his neck.

Bad.

Very bad.

Terrible.

He couldn't figure it out. It couldn't be that he was too old. Hell, he'd just turned all of eighteen. No matter how much loving-around you did, you didn't get too old for it at age eighteen. It was senseless.

What was he supposed to do? Travel? Take a vacation? He'd

just done both of those things and now he was up the creek in a lead canoe. An impotent gigolo. You didn't get rich that way.

So what was he supposed to do?

He went to the library and read up on impotence. All he could find was that it was almost exclusively psychological, which was something he had already figured out.

Chapter 7

"Hold on," he said. "Right here is good enough."

"This is only 93rd," the cabby said. "Thought you wanted 96th Street."

"This'll do."

He passed a bill to the driver, told him to keep the change, then opened the door and swung out onto the sidewalk. It was a bright, warm day—no clouds, a hot sun overhead. For several moments he stood still on the sidewalk, watching the cab pull away from the curb and continue north on Broadway, looking the old neighborhood over to get the feel of it once again after three or four months away from it, sniffing the air and getting his bearings. Then he crossed Broadway at the corner, then continued uptown toward 96th Street with his arms swinging at his sides.

The same old neighborhood, he thought. The same buildings, the same people. He wondered what he'd expected to find. Nothing much, he thought.

Why come back at all? That was a good question. The books would have dozens of answers. Symbolic search after his vanished past. A back-to-the-womb movement. An unconscious attempt to regain his previous footing now that he was slipping.

Hell with it. He was coming back to have a look at his old

stamping grounds. To hell with the books. That was all he was doing and to hell with it.

He wore the jacket of his brown tweed suit with a pair of soft brown flannel slacks. He wore a tan sport shirt open at the neck. He walked easily, but as he approached the pool hall he felt his stride changing to the walk of the old Johnny Wells. He was turning into a jungle animal again, walking hungry. He felt old familiar lines of tension and wariness return to the corners of his eyes and to his mouth.

Home, he thought. He grinned wryly to himself and pulled open the outer door of the pool hall, then took the stairs two at a time. He was still in good shape—good living hadn't ruined his physical condition at all. He hesitated at the top of the stairs, glanced through one door at a small bowling alley, then opened the other door and strode into the pool hall.

Nothing was changed. Cigarette butts were sprinkled across the wood board floor. A gnarled man stood behind the counter and smoked a cigar. Teen-agers leaned against the walls, bent over the green felt-covered tables, smoked and talked. Older men played billiards with the precision of mathematicians. It took Johnny a couple of seconds to get his bearings. He hadn't been in a pool hall since he had left the neighborhood. A gentleman didn't frequent a pool hall. A gentleman didn't play pocket pool at all and if he played billiards it was in a home or a private club. He felt awkward standing there and covered his awkwardness by lighting a cigarette. He blew out smoke and felt a little more at home.

He looked around. There were plenty of familiar faces but he couldn't put names to any of them. Ricky and Beans and Long

Sam were not around. He glanced at his watch. It was almost five. Maybe someone would drop around soon.

He walked to the counter and the gnarled man looked up at him. "Gimme a pool table," he said. The man nodded shortly and told him to take table six.

He walked over to select a cue and thought that it was funny—he hadn't said *I'd like a table* or *A table please*. Instead his speech had found its way back to four months ago. It fit the neighborhood again. Funny.

He found a heavy cue that didn't seem to be warped. He rolled it on table six and saw that it was true. He racked the balls tightly, chalked his cue and broke the pack. He walked around the table, getting his bearings, then took an easy shot at the six, trying to poke it into the side, and miscued. He topped the cue ball and it dribbled off the side for a scratch.

He cut his next shot too thin and missed the pocket a full six inches. He shot several more times and missed each time, and he felt as though everybody in the place was staring at him. This he knew at once to be patently ridiculous. Few people at a pool hall waste their time watching other players. But he was embarrassed and more than a little disgusted by the way he was playing. He stopped to light another cigarette and smoked for a few minutes while studying the table and trying to settle down. Then he ground the cigarette under his heel and picked up his cue again, crouching over the table.

He sank two in a row, missed a tough bank shot, dropped another ball, then missed twice in a row. He kept playing and gradually his game came back to him. He still knew how to play—it was just a question of restoring the lines of communication between his brain and his hands. Piece by piece the lines returned. His cuts were more precise, his English better, his position more nearly accurate. He ran a string of five balls climaxed with a tough combination shot and felt a lot better.

He went on playing. The game took control of him—once he got better he stopped worrying about the people around him, about himself, about anything other than the game. He cleared the table, racked the balls, cleared and racked again and again. From time to time somebody approached him and suggested a game; each time he dismissed the new arrival without raising his head and went ahead with his practice. He did not get particularly good but then he had never been top-flight. He could give Beans a game and could take Long Sam most of the time but he was never a match for Ricky. He simply wasn't that good.

He lost track of the time and merely played. Then, while he was lining a hard shot and gauging his position at the conclusion of the shot, a hand took hold of his cue. He whirled around, angry, and Ricky was there.

"Cool," Ricky said. "You're a stranger here. Welcome home, man."

"You been around long?"

"Ten minutes. I been watching you. Man, I never saw you work so hard on a string of balls in my life. You were almost sweating, man. You weren't so bad, come to think of it."

"Just out of practice."

"Yeah, I guess. What are you doing here man? Thought you were gone for good. I was digging the threads, you know, and they stack up fine. You dress like money. What are you doing uptown, huh? Slumming?"

The tone was banter but Johnny caught a note of reproach. "Just wanted to drop around," he said. "See people, like that. What's happening?"

"Not much."

"Beans and Sam around?"

Ricky shrugged. "Beans lammed," he said. "Two, three weeks after you split. Somebody tipped him they saw fuzz around his building. Beans didn't even try to go home. He had a roll stashed and he grabbed it and split. Caught a rattler for Chi."

"He still in Chicago?"

"I don't know, man. Like he never wrote."

"And Sam?"

Ricky sighed. "Sam got busted," he said. "He hit this cat and this cat got a look at his face before the lights went out. Picked Sam out of a lineup. We found Sam a lawyer who told him to cop a plea. He got a year and a day. His lawyer put the fix in for him and he should be on the street in another, oh, three months at the outside. Makes a total of six months."

"That's hard."

"It's a bitch."

"And you?" Johnny looked at him. He looked the same—the same clothes, the same hungry look. But it was always hard to tell what Ricky was thinking.

"I'm alive. You want to split, talk over a beer or something? This place can get on your nerves after a while."

"Solid."

Johnny returned his cue to the rack, went to the counter and paid for his time. He'd been there almost two hours. It hadn't seemed that long.

They went down the stairs to the street, then around the corner and across 96th Street to a small neighborhood bar. Ricky ordered two glasses of draft and they carried them to a table. Johnny sipped the beer and didn't like the taste. But he couldn't order cognac in a bar like that. It would be definitely the wrong way to come on. He sipped more of the beer, then lit another cigarette and gave one to Ricky.

"So?"

"I don't know," Ricky said. "It's a hassle."

"There's a shortage of marks?"

"Not that. But you get a reputation. You hustle too long and they know you, see you coming. I can't get a game around here unless it's with some dumb schmuck who just blew in from Toledo or something. I been going up to a few places in the Bronx, neighborhood places up there where they don't know me. Another week or two and they know me there. It's a bitch."

Johnny didn't say anything.

"Anyway, another two weeks and it doesn't matter."

"How's that?"

"The army. I'm going in."

"You get drafted?"

"Hell, no. They don't draft you until you're past twenty-one around here. No, I signed up. Three years working for old Uncle Sam."

Ricky made circles on the table top with the beer glass. He made half a dozen circles while Johnny sat and watched him. "I don't know," he said. "I figure it'll be a drag. But it's like more of a drag sitting around on your butt all the time, looking to hustle some schmuck for a couple of bucks, then taking in a movie or some dumb broad with braces on her teeth and her eyes crossed. At least I get out of this crap town. Three squares a day, a nice pretty uniform to get the broads nice and hot. Maybe I'm nuts, I don't know."

"It makes sense."

"That's how I figure it but I might be wrong. How about you, man? Got things going for yourself?"

"I get by."

"You must to dress like that. Those threads cost somebody money, man. You working?"

"Still hustling." It was true enough, he thought. He was still working the angles. The money didn't make him any less of a hustler.

"Working the broads?"

"Uh-huh."

"It's a living. I guess it's breaking right for you, huh? That's all that counts."

Johnny nodded. Rick picked up his glass, finished his beer. "Look, man, like I got to go now. I'd like to hang around but I have to cut."

"Something cooking?"

Ricky hesitated. "You remember a girl named Elaine Conners?"

Johnny remembered the girl vaguely and nodded. He tried to recall whether he had made her or not and decided that he hadn't. She wasn't too much to look at. Not ugly, but sort of plain-looking. About a year younger than he was.

"Well, I been seeing her lately. I got to run over to her place now."

"You getting much?"

Ricky looked slightly embarrassed. "Well," he said, "no. It's not like that. I mean she doesn't want to, well, to put out. I suppose she would if I wanted her to bad enough but I don't want to push, if you know what I mean."

Johnny nodded.

"The army bit was her idea," he said. "To get it out of the way, so I won't have to go later. And partly to get some money saved up." He lowered his eyes. "Maybe I'll never see her again, I don't know. But it looks like we might get married or something when I get out of the army. Hell, it's too far away to talk about it. But you never know."

There was an awkward moment during which neither of them said anything. Then Ricky stood up, grinning. "Take it slow," he said. "We'll run into each other, man. Be cool and keep taking good care of the broads. Knock off one or two for me, huh? Just for old times sake."

Johnny watched him leave. Then he turned his attention back to his beer. He looked at it but didn't drink it. He lit another cigarette from the butt of the one he was smoking and thought about Ricky.

Things had changed.

Beans was gone, headed for Chi the last anybody had heard. Long Sam was doing a bit in jail with three months to go before he hit the street again. Ricky was ready to put on a uniform and play soldier. And thinking about getting married to a girl who wouldn't even spread for him.

Things had definitely changed.

And here I am, he thought. Looking around for something

and not knowing what it is. He didn't fit this neighborhood any more. He could relax in it, could let his speech find its way back to the way it had been, could walk like a hood and think like a hood. But it was temporary. He didn't belong on the upper west side any more. He was a different person than the Johnny Wells who had lived on 99th Street.

Where *did* he belong?

A good question, he thought. He picked up his beer, raised it to his lips, then changed his mind and returned it to the table. He just plain didn't like beer. There didn't seem to be any point in faking it.

He stood up and walked out of the bar. He had a problem and he couldn't find the answer. But the answer had to be somewhere uptown. He was fairly sure of it.

Outside, the air had a chill in it. He buttoned the brown tweed jacket. He started to put the collar up the way you did on the upper west side when the air was cold. Then he remembered that it was an expensive jacket and left it as it was.

He started walking after a few seconds of indecision. He had no goal in mind. He simply followed his feet, letting them take him wherever they wanted to go.

He was surprised when he looked up suddenly and found himself standing in front of the building where he used to live. He had not planned on going back. There was nothing to go back to—his room had undoubtedly been rented time and time again since he left it. There was nobody there whom he wanted to see.

Then he remembered the girl.

The fourteen-year-old one. The virgin. The girl it had been so much fun to make love to, and the girl it had been so amazingly easy to forget along with the neighborhood and the old way of life that went with the neighborhood.

Now he remembered her, remembered her and wondered what she was like now, wondered what she had been doing and how she looked and other things about her. What had her name been? Linda, he remembered And her last name had been something unpronounceably Polish, and she lived across the hall from his old room with her alcoholic mother.

Was she still there?

Probably not. But it was worth a look, he told himself. He opened the door to the building and walked into the foyer, with cooking smells hitting his nostrils instantly. It was the same building—it looked the same and it smelled the same. He climbed four flights of stairs and passed all the different odors until he was on the fifth floor. Then he found her door, stood awkwardly in front of it for a second or so, and then knocked.

He waited.

The door opened. A fat old woman with broken blood vessels in her nose opened the door and stood staring at him. She was indescribably ugly. She was also Linda's mother.

"Wanna drink?"

He did not want a drink. "Uh . . . is Linda around?"

"She don't live here."

"Aren't you her mother?"

"Yeah, I'm her mother. What good it is to me, I'm her mother. Yeah."

"She moved away?"

"Ungrateful little slut," the woman said. "She don't live her no more."

"When did she move?"

"I don't know. Yesterday, a month ago, last year. I don't know when. Go away."

The woman's breath was knocking him out. He moved away but kept one foot in the door.

"You know where she lives now?"

"Don't know," the woman said. "Don't care. You want a drink? Get the hell out."

He got the hell out, glad to get away from the woman. He hurried down the stairs and out of the building and wondered why he was disappointed that Linda hadn't been around. She wouldn't have done him any good. The only sensible thing to do with her was to take her to bed, and he couldn't very well do that in his present state of impotence.

He didn't have any place else to go, unless he wanted to head back to the Ruskin and call it an evening. Somehow that didn't appeal in the least. He gave up trying to think straight and sat down on the stoop waiting for something to happen.

Something happened.

She said: "Hello, Johnny Wells."

He looked up and saw her. It took him a minute to recognize her, mainly because he didn't believe his eyes. She was wearing a black skirt that was tight on her hips and a white sweater that was even tighter on her breasts. A splash of lipstick reddened her mouth.

It was Linda.

"Let's go someplace," she said. "I don't like to hang around the building if I can help it. I don't want to run into the old lady. She's worse than ever."

"I saw her a few minutes ago."

"Yeah? How come?"

"I was looking for you."

"I suppose I should be flattered," she said. "One night with me and you disappear for four months. Then you come looking for me and I should be flattered."

"I'm sorry," he said.

"Don't be. You had things to do. I know all about it."

"Yeah?"

She nodded. "You've been making the gigolo scene. Doing good at it according to what I hear."

"How did you find out?"

"I didn't put detectives on you. You hang around this neighborhood long enough and you hear everything about everybody. You know that. Somebody saw you and told somebody else. The word spread. Congratulations."

"Look," he said, "about that night. I'm sorry I left that way. It was a rotten thing to do."

"Forget it."

"I mean—"

"You were the first," she told him. "You weren't the last. So forget it."

He didn't say anything. They were walking east on 98th Street by now and she was holding his arm. He tried to figure her out. She was still fourteen, he remembered, but she wasn't the way he remembered her. She seemed at least several years older. He wondered what had happened to her.

"You don't live with your mother," he said finally.

"Good thinking."

"When did you leave?"

"Three weeks ago. I couldn't take it any more. She got worse every day, drinking like a fish and hollering all the time. If I brought a guy up she raised hell. I couldn't stand it so I cut out on my own."

"Where do you live?"

"Another block the way we're heading. I got a room to myself. It's not much but it's better than the other dump."

"How do you make money?"

"How do you think?"

Her eyes challenged him and he turned away. It seemed somehow inconceivable, but there was one answer and only one. No wonder she seemed so much older than before.

"You hustle," he said.

"Sure. I'm not a professional or anything. I turn a trick when I'm broke. It pays the rent and keeps me eating and that's about all. I don't turn more than a trick a night and I don't work all the time. I'm not a full-fledged whore yet, is what I'm trying to say."

He didn't have anything to say to that. Somehow it seemed very wrong to him that she was playing the prostitute, even on a part-time semi-pro basis. He wondered what kind of a double standard he was dreaming up. If it was all right for him to make love for money, why was it wrong for her?

"Here's where I live," she said. "Why don't you come up for a while?"

"Well—"

"Come on," she said. "It's a clean place. You won't get your clothes dirty or anything. And if we wind up in bed I won't charge you a penny. Old time's sake and all."

He felt that she was laughing at him. Well, maybe she had a right to. He followed her into the brownstone and up one flight of stairs to her room.

"Better than 99th Street," she said. "No smell here. And only one flight of stairs to climb."

She opened the door. It was a small room but she had it fixed up nice. The furniture was old but presentable.

"Nice place," he said.

"You like it?"

"Sure."

"But your place is nicer, isn't it? I'm sure it is. Where are you living now, Johnny?"

He told her.

She whistled. "Fancy," she said. "What does it cost you to hang out there?"

"Thirty-five a week."

"It costs me ten. I guess your place must be pretty slick, huh? 'Cause this isn't bad and yours is three and a half times as much."

He didn't say anything.

"Can I make you some coffee? I'm not supposed to cook here but I got a hot plate and I can make instant coffee. You want a cup?"

"If you're having some."

"Sure," she said. "I'll just put a pot of water up. Wait a minute."

They talked about nothing in particular while the water boiled. She spooned coffee into two white china cups, poured the boiling water into each cup and stirred with a tin spoon. She handed one of the cups to him and kept the other for herself.

"No cream or sugar. You mind?"

"I like it black."

"Me too. You been gone a long time, Johnny. What have you been doing with yourself? You act different. You don't fit in around here any more."

"I know."

"Tell me all about it," she said. "About the places you been and the things you did."

"It's not much of a story."

"But I'm interested."

"Why?"

"Because I like you."

He hesitated, then started to tell her what he'd done, the plans he had made and the way he had carried them out. He started out intending to summarize everything briefly and get it over with in a hurry, but something stopped him from carrying this plan to completion.

Instead he wound up giving her a very detailed picture of his activities from the morning he had left her to the present. Somewhere in the middle of it he began talking as much to himself as to her. It was a way of looking back, a way of getting the whole picture again. He sat in a straight-backed chair and she sat on the bed. He sipped his coffee from time to time and he talked. She listened without saying a word.

He didn't tell her that he'd been impotent lately. He left this tidbit of information out. It was just about all he left out, however.

When he finished they sat in silence for several minutes. He could hear the wind outside. It was blowing up a storm and looked like rain.

"You happy, Johnny?"

"I don't know."

She nodded. "I'm not," she said. "But I don't figure to be happy. I mean, I haven't gotten any place or anything. I live from one day to the next and I sort of bide my time, if you know what I mean. I haven't got any education like you do. I think a lot, but I haven't got much to think about. And I can always tell myself that one of these days something'll happen, a rich man'll come and want to marry me or a million dollars'll fall down and hit me on the head or something. You know what I mean?"

"I guess so."

"So it must be worse for you. I mean, I haven't got anything. If I'm not happy I can still think it's going to be different and I'll come out smelling like a rose. But you've got plenty. Just what you wanted. Don't you?"

He nodded.

"So if you aren't happy it's a mess," she said. "That's what I mean."

More silence. She was right, he realized. She had hit it on the nose. It was bearable when you had nothing, because then you knew that your life was ahead of you and you could only move in one direction—up. And it was better yet when you were moving and you got further along every day and you had something you were killing yourself to get.

But once you got where you were going, then it was time to

watch out. Because then you were in a bind. You could only go one way—down. And you didn't like it so much where you were, and it was a mess.

"Johnny?"

He looked at her.

"I'm not working tonight."

He didn't get it.

"I'm not working tonight," she repeated. "I only hustle when I have to. The rest of the time I just sit around. Tonight I'll just be sitting around."

"Oh," he said.

"And I get lonely. Do you ever get lonely, Johnny? Probably not with all the things you got going for you."

"I get lonely."

"Honest?"

"I don't know anybody. Not really. Unless I'm ... working ... I just stay by myself."

"It sounds like a drag."

"It is."

"Johnny?"

He waited.

"Would you like to stay here tonight?"

He thought about himself and thought about the fact that he wouldn't be able to make love to her. But she hadn't even asked that. She asked if he wanted to stay, and he did want to stay even if he had to sleep on the floor. It seemed very important for him to be with someone this night. It was not entirely a sexual thing. It was more a matter of companionship.

"Yes," he said. "I'd like that very much."

She smiled. "Just sit where you are," she said. "I'll make some more coffee. Then we can talk some more."

It was late. They'd had many cups of coffee and they'd talked about many things. He told her some of the places he'd been to and some of the things he'd done and people he'd met. He told her about things he read in books and things he learned and she listened most receptively. She talked, too, and he was interested in what she had to say.

Then it was time for bed.

"Johnny—"

She was standing now, a strange expression on her face.

"Johnny, sex is a business for both of us. You make more dough at it than I do but we both hustle ourselves for a living. So this is going to be silly, I guess. A busman's holiday. But would you like to make love?"

I want to make love, he thought. It's just a matter of communicating that desire to something that hasn't been listening to me lately.

And he walked to her and took her in his arms.

"Let's leave the lights on," she said. "Like the first time. Remember?"

"I remember."

"Then kiss me."

He hadn't kissed a girl and meant it in a long time. He took her in his arms, felt the incredible softness of her warm young body against him, and his tongue darted into her mouth. He tasted the sweetness of her and his arms held her very close and very tight. His heart started to pound.

"Be gentle with me," she was whispering. "Nobody's ever gentle any more. Nobody's nice or sweet or anything. Be gentle with me, Johnny."

He lifted her in his arms and put her on the bed. He stretched out beside her and kissed her again. His hands found her breasts and he held onto them and felt how soft and firm they were.

"Nice," he said.

"Nicer than last time. They keep on growing. Are they too big?"

"I can't tell."

"Why not?"

"You've got too many clothes on."

"But no bra, Johnny. Just a sweater, see? I still don't need a bra. No matter how big they get they still stand up all by themselves."

"You've still got too many clothes on."

"Then do something about it."

He pulled the sweater over her head, threw it to the floor. When he caught sight of her breasts he had to stop. They were the most perfect he had ever seen. She was right—they had grown since he'd first made love to her. And they were firm, rich and firm, and he couldn't keep his hands off them. They were cool to the touch and the nipples were suffused with desire a second after his fingers touched them.

"See? They're still sensitive."

"Do they like to be kissed?"

"Try them and see."

He bent to kiss her breasts.

Maybe it was going to be all right, he thought. Maybe this time it would work for him. Maybe he would get excited, and then maybe he would be able to make love to her, and then maybe he wouldn't be impotent again for the next fifty years. Maybe she would cure everything.

He hoped so.

But he didn't care simply because he wanted to be cured, simply because he wanted to make love to other women and grow rich in the process.

Not now.

Now only one thing was important. Now he wanted only to make love to her properly and efficiently and spectacularly. Now all that mattered was what the two of them were going to do now, in her bed, in the next hour or so.

Nothing else mattered.

He wanted her more than he had ever wanted a woman in his life. He wanted her badly, so badly he would have given anything for her.

And she wanted him.

"Johnny," she moaned. "Oh, God, there wasn't anybody like you. The others were a waste of time, the others were nothing; there was always you and nobody else. Nobody ever made me feel like this, Johnny. Nobody ever. You're the only man who can make me feel like this."

"How do you feel?"

"Like a goddess."

"That's how you should always feel."

"Why?"

"Because you *are* a goddess."

Her hands were busy with the buttons of his sport shirt. He'd taken his jacket off earlier, when the room had grown warm, and now her hands were inside his shirt, toying with his chest. He kissed her mouth, then moved lower to kiss her breasts again. He touched her leg at the knee and his hand began to travel.

She moaned softly.

"Johnny!"

He took her skirt off.

He looked at her, saw the naked perfection of her body, saw every bit of her.

And something began to happen.

He didn't believe it at first. He had thought that it couldn't happen, that it perhaps would never happen again. But it was happening, and it was happening to him, and he couldn't have been more pleased by any occurrence.

He was a man again.

He stood up, tearing his shirt off, kicking off shoes and socks and pants.

Then he was naked and she was nude and it was time.

Time to make love.

It was magnificent.

No one could tell it in detail because the details were far too subtle to be told. Everything happened, and everything happened quite flawlessly, and the experience for both of them was not only the quintessence of physical satisfaction but a mental and even spiritual experience at once.

When it was over she cried. He did not cry but wanted to, and he held her in his arms, stroked her face and loved her.

Chapter 8

"I'm afraid," she said.

He was lying on his back in her bed and she was lying in his arms, a warm bundle of soft curves. He rubbed her back with one hand while he looked up and studied the cracks in the ceiling. His mind refused to work. It was spinning dizzily. He still couldn't fully comprehend the reality of what the two of them had experienced together. It was too large for him.

"Don't be afraid."

"I can't help it. Johnny, this was like nothing in the world. It was too good, Johnny. Much too good. It was the sort of thing everybody dreams about and reads about, and it was the sort of thing that never really happens to anybody, and I'm afraid."

"Why?"

"I just am."

"Tell me about it."

She sighed. "Because it was too good," she said. "Because I'll lie here thinking it was too good and feeling wonderful about it and then we'll fall asleep—"

"Wrong."

"Aren't you going to sleep here? I thought you would. I mean, you can't go back to the hotel—"

"I'm sleeping here."

"But—"

"Before we fall asleep," he explained. "We're going to do it again. At least once. Maybe twice."

"Oh. Sure, of course. I was planning on it." She giggled, then grew sober again. "But finally we will go to sleep, you know. And then I'll wake up and you'll be gone and I won't see you again. That's the way it will happen."

"Wrong."

"Really?"

"Really."

"You don't have to stay, Johnny. I'm not just saying that. I mean it. And I'd like to say that if you're not here in the morning I'll never let you get near me again, but I can't say that because it wouldn't be the truth. You can have me any time you want me. All you have to do is ask."

"I'll stay because I want to."

"Why? Because you like the way I behave in bed?"

"That's one reason. You're a tiger."

"I'm good?"

"The best in the world."

"I guess you ought to know, huh?"

He couldn't help grinning. "Would you want a man who didn't know anything about it?"

"I guess not."

"Then shut up. Yeah, you're good. But that's only a small part of it. There's more to it than that. There's something else that's a lot more important."

"What's that?"

He took a deep breath. He was about to say something he had

never said to a girl, something he had never felt before. But there was no getting around it now. It was the truth—he was positive of it.

And he wanted her to know.

"It's very simple," he said. "Nothing complicated about it at all. I happen to be in love with you."

"Say that again, Johnny."

"Starting with *It's very simple*?"

"You know what I mean."

"I happen to be in love with you."

She stared into his eyes, her own eyes very wide. "You don't mean that. You can't possibly mean it. You're just talking."

"I mean it."

"It's impossible—"

"But it's true."

"I don't believe it," she said, as much to herself as to him. "A gigolo and a whore in love. I just don't believe it. I don't believe anything."

"You better believe it."

"Johnny, what are we going to do?"

"We're going to make love."

"I mean after that."

"First things, first," he said, taking her in his arms. He kissed her, a long deep kiss.

Then she didn't ask any more questions.

She had better things to do.

•   •   •

The man was named Arthur Taggert. He was seated in a swivel chair behind a sixty-inch oak executive desk. He was between thirty-five and forty years old, and he wore a gray sharkskin suit something like Johnny's, a white-on-white shirt, a patterned gray tie and heavy horn-rimmed glasses. He had a tan which had been acquired via the sunlamp route and good muscle picked up through weekly trips to a gymnasium.

"John Wells," he read aloud. "Age 25. Born March 10, 1936, in Cleveland. Graduate of Clifton College in Clifton, Ohio. M.A. from Western Reserve University. No previous business experience. That sums it up?"

"That's about it," Johnny said.

"Well, you haven't had a hell of a lot of experience," Taggert said. "Just college, and that doesn't really let you know what the real world's like. Sort of an academic fishbowl, so to speak. Too many graduates come to us still so wet behind the ears that all the towels in Manhattan wouldn't get 'em dry. Generally I'll take hard business experience any day of the week. But I just might make an exception in your case."

Johnny didn't say anything. Taggert was head of personnel at Craig, Harry and Bourke, a small but dynamic advertising agency with offices, inevitably, on Madison Avenue. Johnny was applying for a job. He didn't want to get stuck running copy for six months to see if he could make the grade. He wanted to fall right into a copywriting job.

"These samples of yours," Taggert went on. "Now most college boys just don't see what advertising is supposed to do. They use their words right and their grammar is flawless but the end-product is rotten. You can't teach someone to be an ad man. They can learn, but you can't teach 'em. Too much of advertising is intuitive. You have a feeling for it or you don't. I think you've got the feeling. Your copy isn't professional or even close to it, but it's got punch; you're writing an ad, not a goddamn poem for *One Magazine* or something. You'd be surprised how few college types can figure that out."

"I'm glad you like my copy," Johnny said.

"I like it enough to give you a job."

"That's what I want. A place to start."

"Well, all it is is a start. A hundred a week is all I can offer you, but the job'll be writing copy, not carrying it around from one room to the next. You'll get a chance to learn the business. And this is a business where the possibilities are limited only by the capacity of the individual. A man with drive and talent can make more money than he could possibly spend. The industry automatically tailors the job and the reward to fit the man. You can stay at five thou a year for life or go up to fifty in a few years. It's up to you."

"I understand."

"You start Monday," Taggert said. "Report to Bill McClintock. He'll show you what you're supposed to do. It may not be too exciting. Fill-in work—words to go with pictures, printed copy in TV commercials, the hack work that has to round out the whole picture. It may look too easy. Don't be faked out. It's not as easy as it looks. If you're any good, we'll be able to tell it from how you handle this stuff."

He stood up. The interview was over.

Johnny walked over 48th Street to Fifth Avenue, then caught a downtown-bound Fifth Avenue bus to Washington Square. He walked through the park and down Sullivan Street to a neat unprepossessing four-story brick building. He climbed the stairs to the third floor, fitted a key in the lock and opened the door. He walked into the apartment.

"I got the job," he said.

She came into his arms squealing jubilantly like the little girl which, in point of fact, she was. He picked her up off the floor and hugged her and kissed her and laughed. "Take it easy," he said. "For Christ's sake, it's all of a yard a week. I used to make more than that in a night."

"But it's a job!"

"Yeah," he said. "It's also a pretty good starting place. I was kind of certain they weren't going to bother checking me out. They fell for the college stuff all the way. And the age. Not even a question."

Her eyes were shining. "They just picked the best man," she said. "That's all. They read the copy you wrote and realized they couldn't get anybody like you in a million years."

"Well—"

"What do you do, exactly?"

"Filler copy. I write around things. I guess. It's hard to say—I don't start until Monday. You know when they have a commercial on television and there are some words you read while the announcer shouts at you? I'll be writing those words to fit. Things like that. Somebody else supplies the idea and somebody else tells me what to write and I grind out the garbage. That's all there is to it."

"It sounds wonderful!"

"It does?"

"Uh-huh. Oh, it may not be the exciting stuff in the world, but when they see how good you are they'll give you something better. See?"

He grinned at her.

The apartment was pleasant and roomy, on a fairly good street in Greenwich Village. They'd moved in just a week ago, two days after their mutual discovery that they were in love. It had been an interesting week.

One thing was obvious to both of them. They couldn't go on as part-time whore and full-time gigolo and expect to get anywhere worthwhile. From where they sat, that road could lead only downhill. Before long they would either fall out of love or just quit because the situation was impossible. And neither of them wanted that. They both felt that what they had was far too valuable to be given up for that.

At first Johnny had wanted her to marry him. It hadn't taken her long to talk him out of that. She was all of fourteen working on fifteen and you had to be eighteen to get married. She couldn't fake the age requirement.

The next best thing, she explained, was to fake being married. People might ask to see a birth certificate, but no one ever asked to see a marriage license. All they had to do was take an apartment as man and wife and live there.

Which is what they did.

They settled on Greenwich Village—they wanted a nice neighborhood at a rental they could afford, and the Village seemed to be the answer. People were pleasant and interesting, the apartment they found was cheap and relatively clean, and transportation to any part of the city was easy.

And they set up shop.

It wasn't all that easy, Johnny knew. For one thing, he had busted his hump to get a job that paid him what he said—less than he earned in a good night. He had seven thou put away and he had clothes bought, but until he proved himself at Craig, Harry and Bourke he would be lucky if they lived on his salary, much less saved a penny. And no matter how much you told yourself that love was the only thing that mattered, it was going to be tough living on a yard a week when you were accustomed to luxury.

It would be tough to eat home or grab hamburgers when you were accustomed to eating in a good restaurant seven nights a week. It would be tough to start counting your change when you were used to letting the pennies go to hell. It was tough to take buses instead of cabs and to walk instead of taking a bus.

Tougher for him than for her. He was used to luxury and she was not. For her, their family income was a high one. For him it was low and he knew it would take him some time to get used to it.

He wouldn't even have looked for the job if it hadn't been for her. From where he sat, it seemed as though any job that was any good at all would be closed to him. But she kept after him, kept telling him how bright he was and how much he knew and how well polished he was in speech and appearance, until she finally made him believe he could pass for a college man on the move.

It took him a day or two to figure out what career would be best. He picked advertising because it was a field where brains and talent were more important than preparation. He had a feeling he might be good in that area, and also it appealed to him in a way. It was salesmanship on a higher level. You took a product and stuck it down the nation's throat, and you did your damnedest to make every man and woman buy the rotten thing whether it was any good or not, whether he or she needed it or not. He thought it might even be fun.

Now he was ready to go.

"I've got dinner ready," Linda said. "You like fish?"

"Sure."

"I made these swordfish steaks. You just fry them in butter and serve them. Wash up and come on in."

He put down the paper and went into the bathroom, washed up quickly and went to the table for dinner. The food was good—Linda cooked well for a girl with no previous experience. But it galled him that she had to cook. A girl with breasts like those shouldn't be frying them over a hot stove. She should have somebody to do the cooking for her. She should eat out at steak houses. She should—

Some day, he told himself. Some day we'll have the whole bit, from a stone house on the Hudson to a Cadillac three blocks long. The whole routine, one of these days.

In the meantime, they had a goal. That was the important thing. When you had nothing to work for, either because you were on the bottom with no drive or on the top with no feeling of satisfaction for what you were doing, then it was bad. But when you were going places you could put up with a lot of crap in order to get where you were going.

They had a goal and they had each other. They were working together, working for something which was important to both of them.

That was plenty.

"Hey, Mr. Phony Husband, was the meal okay?"

"Delicious."

"Did your little old wife do a good job?"

"A great job," he assured her. "Best meal I ever ate. A magnificent meal."

"Do I get a reward?"

"Sure. What do you want?"

She frowned. "I get my choice?"

"Uh-huh."

"Well," she said, "how about a little old toss in the little old hay?"

"You're beginning to sound like a little bit of a tramp, Mrs. Phony Wife."

"If you give me half a chance I'll act like one, Mr. Phony Husband."

He laughed aloud. Then he picked her up in his arms, feeling the familiar surge of excitement that never failed to course through him when he got near her.

He carried her to the bedroom.

"Put me down, you!"

He put her down.

On the bed.

And undressed her.

And undressed himself.

And lay down beside her.

And—

"God," she moaned. "When you do that to me it's like the world is going to end. Being kissed like that drives me out of my mind!"

"I can't help it if your breasts are extraordinarily sensitive, can I?"

"Just shut up and kiss them some more."

He shut up and kissed them some more.

"Johnny," she moaned.

He moved now, ready for her. And she was ready for him, and it was the way it always was with them, the way it had been with them every time they were together, the way it always was and the way it always would be.

It was perfect.

He worked at advertising with the same tenacity and perseverance with which he had attacked the business of being a gigolo. He followed a routine not too dissimilar from the routine he had followed during the days when he lived at the Ruskin and spent every morning at the 42nd Street Library.

They awoke together at eight—or earlier if they intended to spend part of the morning making love. Linda cooked breakfast, while he read the *Times*. Then they ate and he took the bus to the office where he worked like a dog. Then he came home, did some special studying, and they went to a coffee house in the Village to relax or stayed at home and listened to records.

Progress was slow at first, inevitably enough. There were days when he felt he was making no headway at all, days when he was sure everybody else in the business was doing much better than he was. On those days he got tough to live with. He hit moods of depression that were almost unbearable, as much so for Linda as for him.

He wasn't used to failure. Thus far he had succeeded at everything he had tried. In addition, he was fundamentally an eighteen-year-old in a field of grown men. They didn't know how young he was, and he tried not to think about it, but it was inevitable that he would lack the maturity of his co-workers in some areas. And this hurt him, and he knew it.

But, although progress was slow, it came to him. McClintock couldn't help notice that he did his jobs well, displaying a rare combination of imagination and technical competence. He got no promotions and no raises, but he had the feeling that he was first in line when a vacancy opened up. And in the ad game vacancies could open with tremendous speed. He hung on, waiting for the break, and the time passed easily enough.

He worried about Linda. With him working she was left alone eight hours a day, five days a week; left completely alone in a neighborhood where she was a stranger. She knew a few people, friends they had met at one coffee house or another, but they were not that close to her and she spent most of her afternoons sitting in Washington Square or hanging around the apartment. He wasn't worried that she would start an affair with anybody, since he was firmly convinced that she could no more be interested in another man than he could be interested in another woman. It was out of the question.

He only worried that she would be bored stiff, or that things would get on her nerves. But this didn't seem to happen. She was satisfied to share his life and she did this tremendously well. He couldn't complain.

So he worked and he kept going. Whenever things got tough the vision would come back into his mind—the vision of himself and Linda in that big old stone house overlooking the Hudson, with the long Caddy in the garage and maybe a little sports job for her, say a Mercedes-Benz 300SL, parked next to it. And children, he thought. A houseful of kids for her to take care of. It made a pretty picture.

A hell of a picture.

With that picture in his head they could shovel all the mud in the world at him and he could take it. With that picture he had enough drive to push all of them into the background. They couldn't stop him.

Then the picture disappeared.

It happened all at once.

It was a Thursday, and he was on his way home from work, done with the bus ride and heading through the park. He crossed the park and started down Sullivan Street and then he saw the cops standing in front of his building. There were two of them and they were waiting for him.

His first reaction reflected his early years. He thought that he had done something illegal and that they were waiting to arrest him for it. He wanted to turn and run from them but he knew better. But what had he done? Who had complained about what? Would they be able to make it stick?

Relax, he told himself. He hadn't done a thing, he was a solid citizen now, a copywriter with Craig, Harry and Bourke with money in the bank. Nothing was wrong, it was something else, they probably weren't even waiting for him.

"You Mr. Wells?"

"Yes," he said. "Something I can do for you?"

"Mr. John Wells?"

Something was wrong. He could see it in the face of the older cop. Something was very wrong."

"Tell me," he said. "What's the matter?"

"You have a wife named Linda?"

"That's right."

Not really my wife, he almost added. We're in love. We live together. We love each other. You can call it a common-law marriage if you want. You can call it—

The older cop was now looking at his feet. Johnny turned to the younger cop. He, too, was looking at his feet.

"Go ahead," Johnny said. "Tell me."

"It's bad news."

"Tell me!"

"Your wife went to a hospital today," the older cop said. "She had had an abortion. God knows where she got it. Some chiropractor or something. It was a bad one."

"She . . . she wasn't pregnant."

"I guess she didn't tell you, Mr. Wells. Sometimes it happens that way. A wife gets pregnant and she doesn't want to let her husband know about it. Probably figures you can't afford the kid and the best out is to get rid of it."

"How . . . how is she?"

The cop looked away.

"She isn't dead," Johnny said. "You're not going to stand there and tell me she's dead. You can't tell me that. You just can't tell me that."

The cop didn't look at him.

"All right," Johnny said. "She's . . . dead. Now tell me about it, damn you. Tell me!"

The cop took a long breath. "I don't guess there's a lot to tell," he said. "She reported into St. Luke's hospital the middle of the afternoon. Reported to emergency. They rushed to take care of her but she was hemorrhaging and they couldn't stop . . . couldn't stop the blood. She kept losing blood until she died."

How had she gotten pregnant? They'd taken precautions constantly except for a few times when it was supposed to be safe. When had it happened?

Oh, who cared? Who cared about anything?

Linda was dead.

"Who did it? Did you catch the guy?"

"We don't know who did it. Even if we did we couldn't prove it, couldn't make it stick. But one of these days we'll get the bastard. They make a slip and it catches them."

Did that bring back Linda?

"Mr. Wells—"

"How pregnant was she?"

The cop looked at him.

"How long?"

"The doc said three to four months. Anywhere between. It's hard to tell to the day, but—"

He didn't hear the rest. He didn't hear anything, wasn't aware of the formal police interrogation or anything else, because as soon as that single fact registered on his mind the rest of the screen went blank.

Three to four months.

Which meant it wasn't his kid.

That made it add up. That was why she hadn't wanted to have the kid, why she had gone so far as to chance an abortion without telling him a thing. It was a kid somebody had given her when she was earning a precarious living as a part-time prostitute, a kid she had conceived before they had started living together, before they had fallen in love.

She could have told him, he thought. She could have told him. And he would have made her have the kid. Hell, it didn't matter a damn whose kid it was. It was *her* kid, wasn't it? And it would be his kid, too, because he would be its father and take care of it and buy presents for it and be nice to it and take it for walks in the park and—

And it didn't matter now.

Because the kid was dead.

And so was Linda.

He tried to believe it, and then he tried to forget it, and one state was as bad as the next. He tried to imagine what life would be like without her, and he went to the window of the apartment and wondered if a three-flight fall would kill him, and then he realized that he did not have the guts to kill himself.

He didn't have the guts to live, either.

He took all the money in his wallet and all the money in the apartment and he left. He walked along the streets until he came to the first bar he saw, and he went into it, and he ordered a double of brandy.

And drank it.

He ordered another of the same and he drank that one also. He kept ordering brandies and they kept setting them up for him and he kept knocking them off. Whenever he closed his eyes he saw Linda. Whenever he opened them he saw her again—floating on top of the brandy in his glass.

He kept drinking.

When morning came it was Friday and he was supposed to go to the agency but he was too drunk to go. He thought that he really ought to call them and tell them but he didn't feel like it and didn't much care because all he could think about was Linda.

He didn't call

He drank instead. He drank brandy for breakfast and brandy for lunch and brandy for dinner, and he kept on drinking until his money ran out, at which time he went back to the apartment and found things to pawn.

And went on drinking.

Saturday and Sunday passed in a blue blur.

Then Monday came, and once again he was too drunk to go to work.

So he drank.

Chapter 9

He was sitting in a bar on Lexington Avenue in the Fifties and he was drinking cognac. He wasn't sure just what day of the week it was and he didn't particularly care. He was Johnny Wells and he lived at the Hotel Ruskin and that was all he cared about. Anything else was immaterial.

He was Johnny Wells and he was wearing a gray sharkskin suit with white shirt and pearl-gray tie and expensive black shoes, and he was drinking cognac.

He was remembering a girl named Linda.

She was dead, of course. Dead trying to eradicate from her body the seed some other man had planted within her. And he was alone, and this fact made many things unnecessary.

It made the apartment on Sullivan Street unnecessary, because he had known at once that he could no longer live there, not with her gone. The apartment, a pleasant place in a pleasant area that had been their love nest, would be hell without her. It was the perfect place for a man and a woman in love, but it was no place at all for a man alone.

When the first bout ended, when he woke up one morning with a hangover so massive and all-consuming that he thought for the first hour of it that he was wearing somebody else's head, he had managed to get back to the apartment on Sullivan Street.

He washed up as best as he could and shaved himself without cutting up his face too badly. He dressed, packed the few things he wanted to take with him, and caught a cab to the bank. He drew out a few hundred dollars and took another cab to the Ruskin.

They were kind enough to take him back. His old room had been rented but they gave him another just as good and he went into it and took another bath and then went to sleep. He went to sleep. He went out later that day and bought a bottle of cognac at a liquor store. He took it to bed with him.

Now two more months had passed. He had never even so much as considered returning to his job writing copy for Craig, Harry and Bourke. The job belonged to another world, a world where Linda was alive and in love with him. He no longer inhabited that world. The job was part of the goal, the big, happy, beautiful goal which included Linda and their children and the house overlooking the Hudson and the Cadillac three blocks long.

Now there were no more goals.

And no more dreams.

Only Johnny Wells, alone.

And for Johnny Wells alone there was no point in breaking your hump writing copy for a yard a week with a chance for advancement when you could bust your hump half as hard for ten times the dough taking care of widows and divorcees and other men's wives. So it didn't take him long to drift back to the bars on Lexington. He did this automatically. One day the money ran out, and he didn't feel like further depleting his bank account, and that night he went to a bar whose name he since forgot and managed to get himself picked up by a sloppy-breasted woman with incongruously blonde hair. The hair was from a bottle and the woman was strictly from hunger, but Johnny had a job to do and he acquitted himself nobly. He left the woman's apartment with the memory of her loose skin under his hands and with a crisp hundred dollar bill in his billfold. He worked a week to earn that much at Craig, Harry and Bourke. Now he was making that much in a night again.

He sipped his cognac and waited for something to happen. In the days when he was hustling he didn't wait for things to happen. He spotted a likely prospect and worked for his money.

Now he didn't care enough to try too hard. Besides, he was drinking a little bit more than usual and the cognac was beginning to reach him. He was content to simply sit and drink until something came his way. And if nothing did come his way, well, that was all right too. He didn't really care that much. He wasn't going to starve to death. He could afford to bide his time.

He felt very old and very tired. Often he tried to remind himself that he was all of eighteen years old but he could never really believe it. Or was he eighteen? It seemed to him that he'd hit another birthday somewhere along the way, that he was in fact nineteen, but he had trouble keeping track.

It didn't really matter. As far as he could tell, he was neither eighteen nor nineteen. He felt at least forty, sometimes older. In eighteen or nineteen years—did it matter which?—he had done more living than most men did in a lifetime. And it was beginning to show.

He finished his cognac and signaled for a refill. It was funny, he thought. He'd originally switched to cognac as a steady drink for three reasons. One—he liked the taste. Two—it was something a gentleman could drink. And three—he could nurse a drink for an hour and never get drunk.

Funny.

Nowadays he drank his cognac without really tasting it. And the gentleman bit certainly didn't matter—he had other more important things to worry about than his boyish concept of what a gentleman was and what a gentleman did and all nonsensical manure like that.

And the third reason certainly didn't apply. He didn't nurse his drinks any more. He drank them right down, and he got drunk on them.

Funny.

He decided he wanted a cigarette. He reached in his pocket and pulled out a cigarette case, reached in again and got his silver lighter. He took a cigarette from the case and put it to his lips, then flicked the lighter. It lit on the first try, as it always did, and he took the light and drew smoke into his lungs. It tasted foul. Everything did lately.

"Want to hold the light, sweetie?"

He turned and looked at her.

She wasn't bad, was in fact better than he was used to. She was in her thirties but that was to be expected—girls in their twenties got all the romance they wanted without paying for it. This one was holding up well. She had jet black hair swept back into a bun and her skin was firm and pinkish. She still had a shape, too—a nice pair of boobs, unless they were phonies, and a trim waist. He couldn't see her legs and didn't know whether they were good or not.

He lit her cigarette.

"Thanks," she said. "Nice night, huh?"

"Very nice."

"The night is nice and so are you. Busy tonight, honey? Or can we get together?"

Most of them didn't talk like this one. Most of them were subtle as all hell, while this one had half the subtlety of an atomic weapon. He started to resent her, then changed his mind. In a way her bluntness was refreshing. Hell, she knew the score and so did he. Why not call a shovel a shovel?

"Sure," he said. "I guess we can get together."

"It has to be tonight," she went on. "There's a very special party tonight."

There was always a very special party.

"A highly unusual party," she went on. "You've probably never been to one like it."

"I've been to lots of parties," he said.

"Ever been to an orgy?"

That one stopped him. He stared at her, and his expression must have been a riot, because she burst out into hysterical laughter. "Oh, come on," she said. "Let's get out of this inverted whorehouse. I'll tell you about it outside. I think you may kind of like it."

They went out onto the street. It was cold out and he caught them a cab. They got into the back seat. She gave the driver an address on Park Avenue in the Nineties and curled into his arms. He played his role properly, taking her in his arms, kissing her, holding her close.

Suddenly she took one of his hands and placed it under her skirt. "That's right," she said, "that's where I like to be held."

They rode three blocks in silence while she made appropriate purring noises to indicate her approval.

"A wild group of people," she explained. "All of us rich and all of as bored, like it says in the peepshow magazines. Every once in a while we have a meeting and show some movies. Ever seen a movie?"

"I see lots of movies."

"I mean stag movies."

"No," he said. "I've never seen one."

"They're fun," she told him. "Not as much fun as doing it yourself, of course. That's the most fun of all. Nothing quite like it. But the pictures are fun themselves. They sort of set the stage, get a person in the mood."

"You feel as though you're in the mood already," he said to her.

"Really?"

"Uh-huh."

"I was born that way. But to get back to the picture. This one guy has a brownstone uptown, where we're going. There'll be four couples there. Another woman like me—Park Avenue matrons with time on our hands and money to burn is the way the magazines would put it. And two guys, the guy who owns the house and another like him. There'll be a nice little call girl for each of the guys and another gigolo for the other gal and you for me. Eight all told."

"I got a question," he said.

"Go on."

"Why don't you and the two guys go to it and save money?"

"Because they're our husbands. We need a little variety once in a while, sweetie."

That shut him up. She went on to explain the set-up—there were four love seats in the living room, and each couple had a love seat, and they sat on them during the movie. *Sat* was a euphemism—they did whatever they wanted to do.

Then, when the movie ended, they paired off and went somewhere or simply stayed in the living room and kept at it. It didn't make too much difference.

"Sound okay?"

"I suppose so," he said.

"Any questions?"

"Yeah. One."

"Go on."

"What's in it for me?"

"A lot of fun," she said. "The joy of having me a few dozen times. Need more?"

"Yeah."

"Mercenary," she said. "There's also a quick five hundred bucks in it for you. Good enough?"

"Fine," he said.

The living room took up most of the first floor of the brownstone town house. The other "couples" were all on hand when Johnny arrived with the woman, whose name turned out to be Sheila Chase. Her husband, Harvey Chase, owned the brownstone. He had a little trollop on his arm with curly brown hair and mammoth mammaries. Another man, introduced as Max Turner, was escorting a light-skinned Negro prostitute with breasts just as large as those of the little trollop on Chase's arm.

Turner's wife Gloria was standing beside a young man whom Johnny had no trouble identifying as a comrade-in-arms. The kid's name was Lance and he worked the same bars as Johnny.

It was a weird scene if ever there was one. First Max Turner made a little speech, and then everybody took off his or her clothes and stood around naked and unashamed. It gave Johnny a good chance to have a long look at the body of the woman he was going to be with.

She wasn't bad at all. Happily, her boobs were all hers. They had a slight sag to them but nothing any man in his right mind would complain about. And her legs were very good indeed. She had stretch marks on her abdomen that were a sign that she had borne children at one time or other. That sort of bothered Johnny. He couldn't quite see her as the perfect mother. The picture didn't fit.

But he wasn't complaining. Five hundred dollars was more than adequate for one night's work. And the work might even turn out to be enjoyable. There was no way to say for sure one way or the other, but it might be interesting.

He had never seen a stag movie before. Vicarious sex never particularly appealed to him, perhaps because he had had so much first-hand experience along those lines. The only thing similar to watching a stag movie in his experience was when he had watched the lesbian make love to Moira in the hotel room in Las Vegas.

And that hadn't excited him. Instead it had nauseated him, and he had had to throw up as soon as it was over.

Sure. But maybe this would be different. He would have to wait and find out.

Sheila Chase sat down on one of the velvet love seats and he took his seat beside her. The lights went out. A silver screen rolled down from the ceiling and he stared hard at it, waiting for something to happen. He heard Sheila's ragged breathing at his side; it wasn't at all hard to see that she found such movies extremely exciting.

Well, maybe he'd get a kick too. The cognac was still working in his head and he felt almost drunk but not too drunk to function properly. He dropped an arm over her shoulder and let his hand cup her breast. It was very large and he liked the feel of it against his palm. He held it and watched the screen.

The picture began.

TITLE CARD: HOT STUFF.

The motion picture is set in the great outdoors. It opens with a long shot of a scene somewhere out in the country, possibly shot in upper New York State, possibly in some part of California where most movies and starlets are made. The rural scene pans over a stretch of open field to the shore of a small lake.

Long shot of a girl walking across the field to the lakeshore. She is wearing a man's flannel shirt open at the neck and a pair of tight Levi's. The camera follows her to the water's edge, concentrating on her buttocks. They are plump, and she is walking in a burlesque of the typical trollop's strut.

At the edge of the water she stops and turns to face the camera. She smiles.

SUBTITLE: I'M HOT. I THINK I'LL TAKE A SWIM.

This said, the girl begins to undress. She opens the buttons on the shirt one at a time to reveal breasts which the loose shirt had kept well hidden up to this point. The camera dollies in for a close-up of her breasts. She drops the shirt to the ground.

Her hands play with her breasts. The camera watches.

SUBTITLE: I WISH SOMEBODY WOULD DO THIS FOR ME.

The camera moves back. The star of this epic now undoes the belt of her denim slacks, then unzips them and peels them off. She pirouettes for the camera in order to expose all her charms to its omniscient eye.

The camera focuses on her buttocks. She turns again. The camera pans her body from her feet to her waist.

Then the girl plunges into the water. She begins to swim lazily about as the camera watches from the shore.

Now a man comes into view.

He does not notice the girl, nor does he take any note of the girl's clothing. Instead he simply walks to the lakeshore, then turns as the girl did to face the camera. He is a tall, dark, good-looking man with long and neatly-combed black hair. He smiles at the camera.

SUBTITLE: HO HUM. THINK I'LL TAKE A SWIM.

The man begins to undress. He is wearing a skintight tee shirt which he peels off over his head and throws to the ground. He has a good suntan, as if he is in the habit of swimming like this every day of the week. His chest is hard and taut, his arms well-muscled.

The camera moves to one side and the man again faces it, so that his side is to the water.

Shot of the girl's face. She is crouching in the water so that only her face is visible. She is smiling hugely, her eyes wide. It is obvious that she sees the man and likes what she is looking at.

Shot of the man as he strips quickly.

Shot of the man's face.

SUBTITLE: WISH I HAD A WOMAN

The girl swims in toward shore. She reaches the shore and climbs up on the bank, smiling at the man.

Shot of the man. He is obviously very pleased that the girl has arrived.

Shot of girl's face again.

SUBTITLE: DO YOU LIKE ME?

Shot of man, nodding his head YES.

Shot of girl. The camera pans her body. She touches herself, walks toward the man. He reaches out and places his hands on her breasts. He begins to fondle her and the camera closes in.

Johnny was perspiring.

He hadn't expected this. Viewed from a distance, the picture was crude and stupid. It shouldn't be exciting, not to a man who'd literally had more women than he could count. It should be boring from start to finish.

It wasn't.

On the contrary. He wasn't sure why this was possible.

It certainly wasn't that the woman was pretty. She wasn't bad, but he had a better-looking woman on the couch next to him. And he'd made love to many better-looking women in his time.

He guessed that it must be the idea of watching something

forbidden. Something like that, maybe. It was hard to tell, but that was his guess.

Sheila moved beside him.

He saw her face in the half-light. Her mouth was tense with desire and beads of perspiration dotted her forehead. He could smell her as well. She used a great quantity of a very expensive perfume but that wasn't all he smelled.

He smelled *her*.

"Johnny—"

"Come here, baby."

She came to him and he drew her down, pressed his face between her breasts. For a moment it was as if there were two Johnny Wells, one of them on the couch with Sheila Chase and the other standing off at a distance watching and snickering at him. The standing-off one had plenty to snicker at, he had to admit.

Here he was, an experienced guy, a guy who'd been around plenty. Here he was lying on a love seat with another man's wife while the other man was with a cuddly little call girl. Here he was watching a picture of two people making it and getting interested himself.

Well, what of it?

He didn't care about a lot of things now. He didn't care who or what Sheila Chase happened to be. He cared only that she also happened to be a woman, and that at the moment he needed a woman, and that she was handy.

That was plenty.

So he bit her and heard her cry with pain and passion both at once.

"Johnny—"

He looked at her.

"The line from the picture," she moaned. "The line the girl says to him right before they do it."

He waited.

She quoted the line. It had been strange to see those words in print on the screen, and it was even stranger to hear them come tumbling from her lips.

He gave her just what she asked for.

On the screen, the man and the woman finished their first bout of lovemaking. The man is lying flat on his back, scratching himself with one hand. The woman is lying on her side, looking down at him.

SUBTITLE: LET'S DO IT AGAIN.

They both stand up. The camera moves for a side angle as the woman bends down, finally crouching on her hands and knees.

The man moves behind her.

Shot of woman's face, passionate.

SUBTITLE: NOW!

Shot of the man's face, smiling hugely.

The man does it to her.

Finally the man and woman finish.

"I'm ready again," Sheila said.

"You're always ready."

"I'm burning up. But it's the damnedest thing I don't want to stop watching the picture."

"Neither do I."

She was grinning. "I told you it was exciting," she said. "You didn't think it would be. But it is. It's exciting as all hell."

"I know what you mean."

"You too?"

"Uh-huh."

She sighed. "And now I want to make love. I want to keep watching the picture, but I also want to make love. Two drives, each in a different direction. Profound, huh?"

"Sure."

He knew what she meant. He had thought that one session on the love seat with her would take his mind off sex for a while, but the picture was having too great an effect upon him. Once again he was caught up with desire for her. And the picture was still exciting. He didn't want to take his eyes off it if he could help it.

"I have an idea," she said.

"Yeah?"

"I want to watch the picture," she said, "and I want to make love."

"How?"

"You won't be able to see the picture," she told him. "I will, but you won't. I guess that's the price you pay in return for the five hundred dollars. See what I mean?"

He saw what she meant.

"It won't be too great a sacrifice," she said. "You've seen most of the movie already. Now I want you to kiss me while I watch the rest of it."

"I get it."

"You know what I want you to do?"

"Uh-huh."

"And it's fair, isn't it? I don't want you to miss the show but there's no help for it. I'm paying you, after all. Lots of money. Five hundred dollars."

"I understand."

The man and the woman had finished, and they were now both cavorting in the water. The camera examined them in the distance but there was not much to see.

Then a young girl came into camera range. Now the young girl is undressing and the camera is watching her. She is a very lovely young girl and seems to be very young. She wears no makeup and her breasts are small.

She is nude now and the camera is busy examining her body.

Shot of the faces of the man and the woman. They are looking at the girl and they seem interested.

Shot of man's face alone.

SUBTITLE: SHE'S A PRETTY ONE.

Shot of woman's face.

SUBTITLE: WE COULD HAVE FUN WITH HER.

The two of them swim madly for shore. They clamber up on the bank and run for her.

Shot of the girl. She does not seem to know what to do. The expression on her face says that she is frightened but she makes no move to run away.

Shot of man's face.

SUBTITLE: NOW WE'VE GOT YOU!

The man grabs the girl from behind and holds her around the

waist. She struggles but cannot get away. The woman moves in front of the girl and takes the girl's breasts in her hands.
Shot of woman's face.
SUBTITLE: I'M GOING TO HAVE FUN WITH HER.
The woman suits her actions to her words.
The camera has a good time watching this most unusual display.
Shot of man's face.
SUBTITLE: IT'S MY TURN NOW.
The man and the woman succeed in getting the unwilling girl down upon the ground.
The man falls upon the girl and begins to make love to her.
The camera watches.

He was walking.

It was night, a very black night, and he was walking. Five fresh hundred dollar bills were in his wallet. They had not been there before.

They were his to keep. They were his in reward for having participated in the most sickening display of promiscuity he had ever heard about, not to say had anything to do with. They were his, and he had worked hard for them.

He wanted a drink.

The movie ended, and that was just a signal for the rest of the festivities to begin. The festivities had been odd ones. Someone had given him something to drink, something which contained a powerful stimulant, and the stimulant had gotten him through the evening in one piece.

In the course of the evening he had made love, not just to

Sheila, but to every woman around at least once. He had made love in manners not even *he* had had any familiarity with. He had made love in ways that were sickening and disgusting, but he had done everything they had wanted him to do.

Now he was exhausted

He walked down Fifth Avenue alongside of the park. He thought how late it was and wondered why he didn't hop into a cab and go home. Home? The hotel, then. He didn't have a home. The Ruskin was the best substitute available.

A cab cruised hopefully by but he didn't bother to hail it. He kept walking.

Because it occurred to him that there was no point in hurrying to get home. No point at all. What was there when he got there? Just a bottle and a bed—cognac to drink and a bed to curl up and sack out in. That was incentive enough generally, but after what he had been through it was not incentive enough.

Nothing was.

He had arrived. He was a real gigolo now, reputation established, good clothes, money in the bank, the manners of a gentleman.

A gigolo.

And what the hell good was that? For that matter, what the hell good was he? What the hell good was Johnny Wells? The answer was simple.

No good.

No good at all.

I ought to kill myself, he thought. Not because my problems are too much for me. Not because I'm desperately unhappy. Just because there is no point in going on. Just because I'm bored stiff and I'm going to be bored stiff for the rest of my life. How many years left? Twenty or thirty or forty or fifty or sixty?

Too many.

Too many years.

And the years would all be the same. The same damn routine going on and on forever. Oh he could relax now and then, take things easy. He could travel or knock off for awhile, or something. There were loads of things he could do.

They all added up to nothing.

A big fat nothing.

And suddenly he realized he was only nineteen years old... that was it, he remembered; nineteen, definitely... and his life was ended. He had pulled himself up out of a gutter and made something of himself, just once. Oh, not during his gigolo period, which had returned, but during those brief days when he had known a great deal of innocent peace, hard work, simple happiness with Linda. He had put the lie to those who said teenagers could never make a go of marriage. He had, and Linda had, and now neither of them were alive any more. *She* was dead, and he wasn't a man any more, he was simply a nineteen-year-old kid who had been living way over his head in a world full of knees in the groin and fingers in the eyes. Nothing... he was reduced to nothing!

Nothing to do and no place to go and nobody to see. Nothing at all—and that, all in all, was the reason he ought to kill himself. It was simply that there was nothing left to live for, and wasn't that reason enough?

No, it wasn't.

Because there was nothing to die for, either. Right away, when

Linda died, he could have killed himself. Then there might have been a point to it, a reason for it.

But he hadn't had the guts then. And now there was less point to dying than there was to living. So he might as well go on, because there was nothing else to do.

When another cab came by he hailed it and hopped into the back seat. He tried to relax while the cab headed for the Ruskin, tried not to think about Sheila Chase or her sickening husband or anybody else at the party.

It was hard forgetting them.

It wasn't any easier back at the Ruskin. But at least he had the cognac. It let him forget a great many things.

He drank himself to sleep.

Chapter 10

The drinking did it.

It will do it every time. Drink enough, often enough and the world is going to fall in on you. It doesn't matter who you are. It happens every time.

It happened to Johnny. To Johnny Wells, the golden boy who could do no wrong.

It happened to him like a ton of bricks.

Too many nights passed in a fog of alcohol. Too many days passed the same way, and too much money went out while no money came in. When the money goes that way you can bet that the end is not far away. It might have taken a long time, because there was quite a bit of money, but it didn't. The money didn't last that long because he was too drunk to hang onto it.

He managed to get rid of almost all the money at once. It happened in a rather interesting way, and it was funny, if one finds such things amusing.

He woke up one day at eleven in the morning with a tremendous thirst. His hands were shaking and he felt like a mangy dog. He knew the cure, however, because he had been there before. This was nothing new to him. It was just a repetition of the way he woke up every morning, the way he felt every morning. His hangover was the only friend he had and he would have been lost if one morning he had awakened without it.

He knew the cure. He reached out for the brandy bottle which was always by the side of the bed. There was enough in it to take the edge off, which is what he wanted to do. He brought the bottle to his lips and drained it in a single swallow. Not all of the brandy wound up in his mouth. Some of it slopped over his face and wet his beard. He hadn't shaved in several days and his beard was long already, a thick covering of stubble that kept him looking like hell.

The brandy helped

It did part of the trick, anyway. The headache did not entirely disappear, but then it never did. The headache was always with him in one degree or another, a constant reminder that he needed a drink. Because he always needed a drink, from the moment he woke up in the morning until the moment he passed out at night.

There was nothing to do about it but drink. One time he had remembered Ricky, and in a moment of pure desperation had presented himself at the nearest army recruiting office. He figured they could take custody of his mind and body for three years. Maybe they could straighten him out. It was a cinch he couldn't do the job himself.

But they took one look at him, laughed aloud, and booted him out on his tail.

So now he didn't try to fight it any more. His bottle of brandy was empty. He dressed in a hurry and checked his wallet. It, too, was empty. He had to go to the bank again. It seemed as if he was going to the bank every goddamn day of the week. He hoped the bank was open. He was broke, and he couldn't even take a goddamned bus to the goddamned bank, and he had to walk it. Fortunately, or unfortunately, depending upon your point of view, the bank was open.

By this time he was heartily sick of the bank, and heartily sick of making trips to the bank, and sicker still of having an empty wallet and a monumental thirst for brandy.

So he waited patiently in the line, looking out of place among dozens of clean-shaven happy-looking people, and when he was first in line the clerk looked at him as if he was wondering what Johnny could possibly be doing there.

"How much is my bank balance?"

The clerk asked him if he had an account.

He got mad, and he snapped at the clerk, and finally he managed to get across who he was and yes, he did have a cruddy account in the cruddy bank, and how much was in it, you dumb stupid son of a bitch?

The clerk finally supplied the good news that Mr. Wells had on deposit slightly in excess of twenty-seven hundred dollars. Another clerk confirmed that this intoxicated pig was indeed John Wells, and Johnny, sick of the whole thing, drew out his entire account.

It was quite a bit of money.

He tried to go through it like a drunken sailor. He went over to Ninth Avenue, where the bars were all in a row and one worse than the next, and he went into the first bar he came to and ordered a double brandy. He downed it in a single swallow, slapped a ten dollar bill on the top of the bar and told the soiled barkeep to keep the change.

Then he went to the next bar and repeated the process.

Now, when you have twenty-seven hundred dollars in your

kick, it takes you a long time to spend it on liquor. Even at ten bucks a drink, you would have to hit two hundred seventy bars before you were broke.

It didn't take him that long.

Because a man who spends ten bucks on a drink attracts a certain amount of attention. Johnny attracted one hell of a lot of attention, and two fine young citizens followed him and waited for the right moment and then gave him a length of lead pipe in back of one ear.

He went down cold, and when he woke up several hours later with the worst headache and hangover of all his wallet was gone forever. He wasn't particularly disturbed about the money, but the wallet was that alligator billfold he had stolen from Mrs. Nugent, and in a sense that was where the whole thing had started. He was sort of sorry to see the wallet go. He kind of liked that wallet, for sentimental reasons.

It took them four days to kick him out of the hotel. They liked him, and they were sorry to see him go, but you don't let a penniless drunk stay in your hotel indefinitely unless your name is Harry Hope. He went out with his suitcases in hand, and he pawned the suitcases and their contents and got himself a few more drinks.

And that was that.

He traced a regular route, from the Hotel Ruskin to a rundown flophouse on West 47th Street, from that place to a hotel on Bleecker Street, from Bleecker Street to another worse dump in Hell's Kitchen. His taste for brandy died when the money was gone. Brandy was too expensive. Wine was cheaper, even if it did have a more deleterious effect on your system. It got you just as drunk and the price was lower.

It was only a matter of time before he wound up where he had started. Only a matter of time. It made sense to get back to the old neighborhood—the way he was going he was destined to wind up on the Bowery and he didn't want that. Something kept him from hitting the Bowery. It sent him to the upper west side again, where it had all begun, where the whole mess started not that long ago.

How long? A couple years? He didn't know anything about time any more.

Time doesn't matter when you're drunk enough.

The upper west side made sense. There were still a few friends in the area and once in a while he could make a touch. Ricky slipped him ten bucks, which helped tremendously. Beans blew in from Chi another time, back to try his luck in New York again, and gave him twenty. Long Sam was good for a dollar now and then when he wasn't in the can.

And finally he got a job.

It wasn't a real job. It put a roof over his head and a few bucks a week in his hands. He worked as an assistant janitor in a brickfront dump, carrying out the ashes and picking up the garbage. It was the type of job only a drunk would take, and it was perfect for him. He put in a few hours a week, stayed drunk whether he was working or not, and nobody bothered him. He didn't have to worry about rent money because the room was his in exchange for the job. He hardly ate at all so food was no expense. A couple of bucks a day for wine was all he needed, and he could usually manage to scrounge that up.

There were always ways. If he couldn't make a touch, he could steal something and hope he didn't get caught. Or he could go back to his old job, but with a difference.

Men this time.

He didn't like it. He didn't like it when the man offered him five bucks to come up to his room for an hour. But he needed a drink, and beggars could not be choosers, so he went.

This happened once or twice a month. It was always a quick five and sometimes ten, and he was low enough by this time so that he didn't get sick thinking about it. There were too many other things to get sick thinking about, and he couldn't afford the luxury of squeamishness.

Sometimes the memories came.

He would remember the days when he had all that money, and he would tell himself that they had not been good days, and then he would think that they must have been better than the ones he was living his way through now.

He would remember a girl named Linda, and he would picture all the things that might have been, and he would get sick once more.

The wine bottle was always there.

It was always a cure.

He always took it.

My Newsletter: I get out an email newsletter at unpredictable intervals, but rarely more often than every other week. I'll be happy to add you to the distribution list. A blank email to lawbloc@gmail.com with "newsletter" in the subject line will get you on the list, and a click of the "Unsubscribe" link will get you off it, should you ultimately decide you're happier without it.

Lawrence Block has been writing award-winning mystery and suspense fiction for half a century. You can read his thoughts about crime fiction and crime writers in *The Crime of Our Lives*, where this MWA Grand Master tells it straight. His most recent novels are *The Girl With the Deep Blue Eyes*; *The Burglar Who Counted the Spoons*, featuring Bernie Rhodenbarr; *Hit Me,* featuring Keller; and *A Drop of the Hard Stuff,* featuring Matthew Scudder, played by Liam Neeson in the film *A Walk Among the Tombstones.* Several of his other books have been filmed, although not terribly well. He's well known for his books for writers, including the classic *Telling Lies for Fun & Profit,* and *The Liar's Bible.* In addition to prose works, he has written episodic television (*Tilt!*) and the Wong Kar-wai film, *My Blueberry Nights.* He is a modest and humble fellow, although you would never guess as much from this biographical note.

Email: lawbloc@gmail.com
Twitter: @LawrenceBlock
Facebook: lawrence.block
Website: lawrenceblock.com

Made in the USA
Coppell, TX
20 March 2025